Praise for
V

"The Thompson family is loving and supportive and will tease the hell out of you in a heartbeat."
~*Lynda Ryba, Wicked Lil Pixie Reviews*

"If you've never read a Vivian Arend book you are missing out on one of the best contemporary authors writing today."
~ *Book Reading Gals*

"Brilliant, raw, imaginative, irresistible!!"
~ Avon Romance

"This story will keep you reading from the first page to the last one. There is never a dull moment..."
~ *Landy Jimenez*

"This was my first Vivian Arend story, and I know I want more! "
~ *Red Hot Plus Blue Reads*

"Love, loss, and enough heat to have you melting. Vivian Arend brings it all and then some."
~*Kindle Jo Jo, Mama Kitty Reviews*

"HOLY FREAKIN' HELL IS THIS HOT!!!"
~ *Book-A-Holic Anon*

Also available from Vivian Arend

~*~
A full list of Vivian's paranormal print titles
is available on her website
www.vivianarend.com

One Sexy Ride

Vivian Arend

This is a work of fiction. Names, characters, places, and incidents either are the product of the author's imagination or are used fictitiously, and any resemblance to any persons, living or dead, business establishments, events, or locales is entirely coincidental.

One Sexy Ride
Copyright © 2014 by Vivian Arend
ISBN: 978-1-499310-56-6
Edited by Anne Scott
Cover by Angela Waters
Proofed by Sharon Muha

Chapter One

Late June, Rocky Mountain House

DOWN WHERE the wide bend of the river formed a swimming hole, Janey Watson had stripped to nothing but her skivvies. Len Thompson stood hidden in the trees between the gathering by the bonfire and the clearing at the water's edge, and wondered what he'd done to deserve this kind of punishment.

Fading sunlight breached the leafy canopy, shining like a spotlight on Janey's mostly unclothed flesh. Her strong limbs were covered with a nice layer of curves, and she raised her arms in the air, swinging her hips to the music carrying from the distant bonfire.

His body's response was instant and brutal, but escaping his self-inflicted torture was impossible. Nope, it didn't matter that his cock was rock hard. Maybe he could get some relief if he turned his back on the enticing sight of nearly naked Janey and walked away—but that

was impossible. The second option was to yank out his
dick and jack off right there and then.

*Third option—wade in and take what you damn well
want.*

"I can dance forever." Janey shouted to the heavens,
twirling, arms extended like angel wings. Len's gaze
dropped involuntarily over every inch, soaking in the
sight and cursing himself for being too weak to look
away. Firm hips, ample breasts, her hair swinging as she
continued to rotate. Between her legs, a dark patch
showed through underwear that had gone see-through
now that it was wet.

He pressed his hand over his cock. He refused to pull
out his dick and simply give in to the need, but *fuck* if he
didn't want to.

Another grumble of objection rose in his gut as
Shannon and Liz joined Janey, the three girls slipping
into the water and splashing innocently. He was some
kind of goddamn saint for having resisted temptation
this fucking long.

When the girls had snuck away from the gathering
around the bonfire, he'd followed. He'd kept to the
background, but no way, no matter how lighthearted this
get-together was supposed to be, *no way* were three
young women gallivanting off by themselves in the
growing darkness.

And by this point in his life, keeping an eye on Janey
was more than a habit.

If he was honest, every time she barreled into his
personal space with her wild, vibrant energy, he'd been

waiting. Expecting her to be there, tormenting him with her sensual touches and unending flirtation. Even tonight, while she acted as if she didn't know he was watching—her pale skin gone slick with handfuls of river water she laughingly tossed overhead—even tonight he bet anything she knew he was there.

She *always* knew where he was. He knew where to find her.

Like the world's longest game of cat and mouse, he'd avoided taking what she'd willingly offered. Not because the idea didn't make him so hard he had to deal with himself, but because he knew ultimately he couldn't give her everything she needed.

This early in the summer the water was still running cold, and the air was brisk enough that her nipples were hard, clearly visible pressing the front of her wet bra. Len imagined wrapping his lips around them. Sucking. Or biting, giving her the edge of his teeth until she screamed his name.

From the bonfire side of the field, masculine laughter and voices grew in volume, a group of three men joking loudly amongst themselves. The guys had been all over Janey and her friends earlier, and now they left the music and the laughter behind as they moved away from the large gathering of young people and headed along the river.

Here was the reason Len was lurking in the shadows like a hooded vigilante. He'd caught two of their names— Frank and Jerry—but the names were less important than the type. Definitely trouble headed in his direction.

The men all wore wide grins, pausing to drink from the long necks in their hands, laughing as they moved closer to where the girls were.

The out-of-towners who'd joined the party were brash to start with, cracking off-colour jokes as they flirted with the girls. The rodeo brought all sorts of people into town. Great for business, but if the wild sexual energy in the air was any indication, these guys were hoping for more than a few dances.

If the girls were interested, tying one on with the newcomers was their decision. All the girls *except* Janey...

His attitude screamed sheer hypocrisy, but Len didn't give a shit. He'd never liked her flirting or fooling around with other guys, but as long as he didn't have to watch, he didn't have much right to voice an objection.

Tonight? He wasn't letting anyone near her, and he didn't care how fucked up that was.

Frank called toward the riverside, "Hey, darlin', where'd you get to?"

If they kept walking, the men would run right into her. The other girls were nearly as unclothed, but Len found the idea of strangers staring at Janey intensely infuriating.

He pushed off the tree and took to his feet, setting a path to intercept before they made it to the clearing.

Singing burst out behind him as the girls started a very off-key rendition about friends in low places.

"Hear that, Dan? They're looking for new friends. I think we can oblige." One of the dark-haired intruders raised a hand and high-fived his nearest buddy as they sauntered along the grassy edge toward the swimming hole.

Len stepped onto the path at the bend in the river, the last point on the trail before the frolicking party could be seen in all their near-naked glory. He waited silently, arms folded over his chest, his legs spread wide as he lifted his chin and tried to look as imposing as possible. Still ready to react in an instant, because hell, it was three of them to one of him.

He was big, but he wasn't *that* big.

The raunchy comments stalled as the leader of the group spotted Len for the first time. "Well, hey there. You lost?"

"Nope. Figured you must be." Len tilted his head back towards the fire. "The action is that direction."

"There's going to be plenty of action down here soon too," Dan said, bumping elbows with the man next to him as they exchanged dirty laughs.

"I wouldn't bet on it," Len snapped.

Suddenly all three of them were facing him in a line, like a wall with fists. Jerry checked him over more closely, tilting his cowboy hat back before he spat toward Len's feet. "If you plan on keeping all the girls to yourself that wouldn't be fair, now, would it?"

"How much pussy does one man need?" Frank asked, moving to one side as if to shoulder past Len.

Len adjusted his stance to the left, blocking the way. "This pussy isn't up for grabs. Get the hell back to the campfire, and we won't have any problems."

"Oooh," Frank exclaimed. "The ladies got themselves a protector, boys."

"Too bad none of them said they weren't interested." Jerry leaned in and placed a hand on Len's right shoulder. "Besides which, there's only one of you. Just step—"

Len swept his arm up and around, breaking the contact between them. He caught hold of Jerry's arm and jerked it behind his back, turning in a smooth circle to place the stranger between him and the man's friends.

Jerry choked out a cry of pain as Len shoved higher and harder, using his other hand to clutch the man's hair.

"Choose. Go back to the fire, or I package you up and you go home bleeding." He didn't mean to sound dramatic, but when it came to Janey, he didn't have much tolerance.

The cowboys obviously weren't used to fighting together. Their lack of experience was the only thing that saved him because when Frank swung, Len had plenty of time to jerk his human shield into place, the body-shaking blow smacking hard into Jerry's gut.

Len got ready to make his point about leaving a whole lot clearer when nearby feminine laughter jerked him to a stop.

The two men opposite him retreated. Len let Jerry go, shoving the man into his friends.

Thank goodness they backed off, because a second later a wet body was pressed to his back, slim arms tangled around his waist. A far too familiar voice sounded as Janey playfully poked her head around his torso. "Who are your friends, Len? Introduce me?"

Jeez. She sounded shit-faced drunk, but he hadn't seen her toss back that much alcohol. "Go back to the swimming hole, Janey. I'll take care of these guys."

"Uh-uh. I know them."

Damn if she didn't step forward, seeming oblivious that she was damn near naked.

Janey lifted a hand and pointed at Frank. "He brought me a drink."

She smacked her lips and made a funny face before stumbling. Len caught her before she could fall, pulling her soft body against his and cursing silently.

The assholes in front of him continued to stare, checking her over with far too lecherous intent. "That's right. I'm the nice guy you said you wanted to dance with." Frank held his hand toward her even as his gaze snapped up to meet Len's in challenge. "So, come and dance with me, darlin'."

Fuck, no. "She's not going anywhere with you. Get the hell out of here," Len ordered.

Janey escaped from his arms, squirming away before he could stop her. "Slow down there, big-shot bossy-pants." She tilted her chin higher and smirked, her eyes far too bright. "What if I want to dance?"

"You can dance with me," Len offered.

A burst of amusement escaped her. "Right. That never *ever* happens. You and me on the dance floor? Never in a billion, million years."

7

Frank reached for her fingers. "What? Never dances with you? He sounds like a terrible guy. I'm more than willing to take care of you, sugar."

It took an incredible amount of self-control to not jerk Janey away from the other man. Even as he tried to reason with her, he kept an eye on Dan and Jerry, who were moving in dangerously close. "Janey. Get back to the girls now."

She twirled and landed against his chest, every inch of her pressed up tight. She tilted her head back and stared into his eyes with a defiant expression. "Don't boss me around. Nope, nope, nope. Ain't gonna happen."

Behind him, Janey's friends continued to laugh, splashing sounds seeming to grow louder as dusk fell. Len didn't give a damn anymore what she'd say about him taking charge. He hooked an arm around her, ready to scoop her up and beat a retreat. It took his full strength to hold her there, supporting her as she suddenly swayed hard.

"Len? I feel funny."

Her hands slipped from around his neck, and he risked a quick peek just in time to see her lick her lips as she rocked against him.

His body rocked in response. Shit. Not the time or the place.

She started singing, dancing in place against his body. Len held on, gritting his teeth to resist the torment. He glanced up to check on the strangers.

In front of him was empty space, the backsides of the men growing smaller as they hightailed it toward the fire.

Good. At least one disaster was over before it got out of hand. The other, though? Was still driving him mad.

Len peeled Janey off his body, directing her back toward the swimming hole. She danced ahead of him, her butt wiggling as she picked her way over the uneven ground.

He was going to hell. That's all there was to it. The thoughts racing through his mind were far too filthy, but he couldn't seem to stop them.

He jerked off his jean jacket in an attempt to cover her. "Shannon, Liz. Get the hell over here," he shouted.

Their laughter changed rapidly to shrieks as the other girls noticed he was approaching. Neither of them was as naked as Janey with their button-down shirts hanging to their thighs, but they still scrambled for their discarded clothing.

"You just wanted to see us in our birthday suits," Janey teased. She turned in front of him, hiding her hands behind her back as he attempted to get her to put his coat on. "I'm not done. I'm going to swim some more," she insisted.

Liz had made her way to their side. The moonlight shone off the water surface, lighting up the grove of trees. Dusk had fallen far enough it was too dark to see clearly, but Len thought her cheeks were flushed red. She looked as if she was going to make a smart comment to cover her embarrassment, but she must have caught a glimpse of his face.

"What's wrong?" she demanded.

Janey gave him no time to answer. She caught hold of her friend's hands and spun her in a wild circle. "Nothing's wrong. We're pixies in the moonlight. We're dancing on clouds." She let go of Liz and grabbed on to Shannon for a twirl before returning to Len.

Damn if she didn't leap straight at him, throwing herself into his arms. Len barely caught his balance before they would have tumbled to the ground.

As it was, he grabbed hold of her butt, his fingers digging in as she wrapped her legs around his hips and cupped his face in her hands.

She stared into his eyes, all wildfire and passion. "You promised to dance with me. Or are you going to run away *again*?"

"Janey. Get off of him." Shannon sounded scandalized. "Oh my God, what are you doing?"

"He promised. And a promise is a promise." Janey shook off Liz's hand. "Go away. I want to dance with Len."

He caught Liz's concerned expression a second before he had to scramble into action. Janey released both her arms and legs at the same time, and only his grip stopped her from hitting the ground. "Jeez, Janey. Careful."

"Time to swim," she shouted, twirling towards the water's edge.

"What the hell is wrong with her?" Liz asked. "She's like a manic on a high."

Len didn't have time to agree with her as he chased after Janey, cutting in front before she could make it into the water.

She smiled flirtatiously, swaying slightly from side to side as she crouched low into a football stance. "You want to play?"

Liz was right—Janey was not acting like herself. Her eyes were too bright and her gaze darted everywhere, as if she literally couldn't stand still. Len stretched his hands to the side to block any attempts at a dash for the water. "It's time for you to go home."

Shannon was approaching from the back. She held up her hands questioningly, but all Len had were suspicions.

With a total lack of self-modesty, Janey closed the distance between them and caught hold of his belt. "You gonna take me home?"

Sweet mercy. Her words came out husky and low, scraping over his already tormented nerves. He glanced over her shoulder even as he wrapped his fingers around her wrists to stop her from playing with his belt buckle. "Shannon, did Janey have anything unusual to drink tonight?"

Liz joined them as well. "Not that I noticed, but..."

She leaned over and whispered in Shannon's ear. The woman's eyes grew wide, and she slipped between Len and Janey. "Let me take a peek at you, hon."

Shannon somehow kept Janey in one spot for long enough to check her eyes, swearing softly as she wrapped her fingers around her friend's wrist to take her pulse.

Len closed the distance to Liz's side. "She's not drunk, is she?"

A simple shake of the head. Liz whispered softly. "You think someone slipped her something?"

"Drugs?" Len glanced back toward the campfire. The cowboys' behavior became crystal clear. "I wouldn't be surprised at all. Only what did they give her?"

Shannon turned Janey to face them, her arm around her friend's shoulders. "Liz, how about you and Janey go for a walk to the trees and back?"

Janey pouted. "I don't want to walk. I want to dance."

"We can skip. That's kind of like dancing," Liz offered.

Shannon waited until the two of them were out of earshot before she spoke. "It's my guess someone is higher than a kite. It should wear off in a few hours, but until then, she's going to be a handful."

"She doesn't seem drunk," Len protested.

"Not alcohol, but a chemical high. If I had to guess, I'd think it was Ecstasy. It's not *that* dangerous, but we do need to keep an eye on her."

Len's fists twitched to go rearrange a few faces. "I'm going after the bastards—"

"Don't bother," Shannon responded. "You have no proof, plus they're probably miles away by now. Be thankful they didn't slip her a roofie, then take off with her when she passed out."

Even the thought of it made his blood boil. "We need to take her home."

"And keep an eye on her," Shannon insisted.

Janey had Liz over by the trees. She was jumping and trying to touch the leaves on the overhanging limbs. Every other leap ended with her on the ground, laughing uproariously.

Taking her home was a good idea before she broke something.

Only Janey was in the middle of a renovation project. "It can't be to her house either. Who knows what mischief she'll get up to in the place."

"Len, it's got to be you." Shannon turned and pinned him with her gaze. "Liz is heading out early in the morning on holidays. I've got a shift at the hospital starting in a couple hours, so I can't stay with her either."

Leaving him as the uncontested babysitter. Heaven and hell. "Are you sure she's okay?"

She nodded, tightening the ponytail holding her blonde hair back. "She'll be fine. She doesn't need to go to the hospital, and I bet she'd prefer not to be hauled in there like this." Shannon made a face. "I could just imagine how people would react to hearing she was on drugs."

Small-town rumour would suck. No way could Janey afford having dirt talked about her, not with her trying to officially make a go of starting her own business. "I'll take care of her."

Liz had scooped up Janey's clothing on their return trip and handed the pile to Shannon. While Janey curled around Len like he was a May Pole, Liz glanced between their faces. "You figure out what's up?" she whispered.

The situation was now unavoidable. Len cursed himself that he hadn't stopped Janey from getting targeted in the first place, but right now was about making sure she was all right.

Nothing more would happen tonight, except him getting bluer balls than usual, but that was his choice. Had *always* been his choice. Bottom-line—she wasn't going to get hurt any further, not if he could help it. Not by him or some unknown jackasses with an agenda, or by hard-nosed snoopy neighbours who would act as judge and jury and accuse her of wrongs she hadn't committed.

He reached out his hand to Janey. "You're coming home with me."

Chapter Two

THE TUBE of toothpaste and the brand-new toothbrush waiting for her on the bathroom counter got a frantic workout as Janey attempted to kill the foul taste in her mouth. And the entire time she scrubbed, she examined her surroundings in disbelief.

She was in Len Thompson's apartment.

Hell, she'd woken up in the man's bed. After her heart stopped racing in panic, confusion had set in. Why on earth was she in Len's place?

She spit and rinsed, threw some cold water on her face and patted dry with the towel she'd found next to the toothbrush. At least now she felt halfway human, but she still had no idea what was going on.

Something very weird had happened, and she wanted to know what. Soon.

As she wandered through his apartment, she racked her brain for the missing details. The bonfire by the river came back, plus sneaking off with Liz and Shannon, but everything after that was a blur.

A granola bar and an orange sat in the middle of the kitchen table, along with her purse. She rummaged around in it until she found her phone, grabbed the food and took everything back with her to the living room.

She hadn't spent a lot of time in Len's place, but she'd been there enough to recognize where she was. She and his little sister, Katy, had been best friends since they were ten years old, and by the time Janey turned eleven she'd already decided Len was dreamy.

Not that she would have known what to do with him at that age. Nope, kind of like dogs chasing cars. Would they…bury it in the backyard, or what? Images flooded in of enormous piles of dirt with bumpers sticking out.

Whoa. That was weird. Her brain was obviously still not awake.

The clock on the stereo said it was ten a.m., which explained why Len wasn't around.

She glanced down at what she was wearing. The oversized T-shirt had to belong to the man she'd spent years chasing. Had they actually done something?

Even with her foggy memories, the answer to that question was crystal clear. The way her head was pounding, she'd hit the bottle hard, and no way would Len have taken advantage of her being drunk. It wasn't him.

Yet here she was, wearing nothing but his shirt.

She bit into the granola bar and chewed a few times as she pondered that detail. Her brain woke up a little, and she checked more thoroughly, running a hand over one hip.

Nothing. But. His. Shirt.

Jeez, she didn't even have any underwear on. Chewing briskly so she could swallow her mouthful, she poked at her phone and waited for Liz to answer her call.

It went to voicemail. Janey popped off the couch with a curse, her head spinning momentarily at the rapid motion. She tried again, this time connecting to Shannon's number.

Voicemail. *Shit.*

She checked the clock and decided to take the chance. Katy would be home, but who knew if she'd be answering the phone with a two-week-old baby in the house.

Katy not only answered, she was damn near frantic. "I couldn't believe it when Len called me. How do you feel? I came over there at seven to keep an eye on you when he left for work, but you were still sound asleep. I swear I just left, not even fifteen minutes ago, because Tanner got fussy and you were still snoring like a log. I didn't want him to wake you."

"You were here?" This got weirder and weirder. "And what did Len tell you, because all I know is I'm not wearing any clothes, and I'm in his apartment."

"No clothes—" Katy paused. "What do you remember?"

"Not a hell of a lot, especially not about the important things. I doubt you're going to tell me Len and

17

me did the dirty deed, because you would've run screaming if that was the case."

Finally a laugh from her friend. "You got that right. No, hon. You didn't tie one on last night. Someone slipped you some drugs."

Someone slipped her—

A momentary rush of fear was rapidly replaced with anger as the grinning cowboy's face flashed to mind. "That *fucker*. I should rip his balls off."

"You know who did it?" Katy demanded.

Janey thought harder, but it was no use. "I got a first name, and I might recognize his face, but beyond that, nothing. You're serious? Someone drugged me?"

"Yeah. Liz and Shannon said they didn't notice anything until all of a sudden you were dancing like a fool. Shannon thought maybe it was Ecstasy."

Panic hit like a rock fall. "Oh, Lord, did I do anything terrible?"

"Not as far as I've heard," Katy rushed to reassure her. "And you know Len would never let anything like that happen to you."

That was true. The man watched her like a hawk even while pretending he wasn't interested. The split between what he offered and what she wanted was a wide chasm. He'd refused to get close.

Which made her current situation even more confusing. "Why am I in his apartment?"

"You had to be watched last night, and Len was the only one who could do it."

Lovely. "Gee, thanks. Sounds like I was the booby prize at the fair."

"Hey, they didn't ask me. Just assumed they shouldn't dump your doped-up ass on me with Tanner not sleeping through the night." Katy made a rude noise. "You're my best friend, and I wouldn't have minded one bit, but I'm glad Len was able to look after you."

"That makes me feel a little better," Janey admitted. "But I'm still confused."

"You were drugged. Which sucks, but it could have been far worse." Katy's concern was clear. "What if they'd...? No. Not even going there. But, hon? You were lucky."

If the only thing Janey had to deal with was a bit of confusion, she'd been *more* than lucky, considering what could have happened. Her imagination was vivid enough there were paths she didn't want to go down, so she consciously pushed away from considering in detail the hell she'd avoided. Deliberately focused on another part of the big picture. "I understand a little better what you felt like, by the way. After you had your accident and lost track of things. A *little* bit, I mean. I lost a few hours. It sucks."

"It does," Katy agreed. "But you'll figure it out." Soft baby noises in the background rose in volume from gurgles to full-on protest. "Listen to the kid. You'd think I never fed him. One sec."

She spoke away from the phone, and Janey waited patiently as her friend cared for her little one.

"Back."

19

"Am I okay otherwise? Do you know?"

"I talked to Shannon, and she said yes. She'll be off shift at noon if you'd like to call her. But otherwise, everything should be fine." The squawking in the background continued to escalate, and Katy laughed softly. "His royal whininess is summoning me. If you feel up to it, come by for lunch."

Janey needed to get moving anyway. "I'll talk to you later."

She let her friend off the line, debating what to do next. Her confusion was still there, but she wasn't terrified anymore.

It was strange being in the man's apartment without him. Even weirder when she realized she would have to borrow something of his to wear home. The jeans and shirt she'd worn to the party were on the table, and it was obvious he'd tried to clean them up, but no way was she putting mud-stained underwear back on.

Embarrassment increased as she realized Len would have folded the garments. The idea of his hands on her bra and panties was not nearly as sexy as she'd thought it would be.

Of course, she'd always imagined the first time he'd handle her clothes would be while she was in them, alert and eager to play.

So much for *that* daydream.

She stood with her hands on his dresser drawer and took a deep breath, bracing herself before tugging it open and peaking inside. When she caught a flash of underwear she slammed it shut.

Third attempt revealed sweatpants, and she grabbed the smallest pair possible. She was going to have to tie a rope around her waist to stop the fabric from falling off her hips.

She tucked all her things into a plastic shopping bag and shoved her feet into her still-wet cowboy boots. Locked the door behind her and marched the seven blocks home at a rapid pace, letting herself in the unlocked back door of the house she'd grown up in.

Inside was a mess. Even though she'd worked hard to keep things as neat as possible, dust and renovations went hand in hand, and piles of new tiles and flooring were everywhere.

Fortunately, the downstairs bathroom was in one piece, mostly. The light fixture wasn't working, but she'd grown accustomed to showering by the light pouring in from the hallway. Janey stripped off Len's borrowed clothing and stepped into the shower, ducking her head under the steamy water.

She closed her eyes and let the heat soak in. Well. That hadn't been the kind of morning she'd expected.

Janey opened her eyes and stared forward, concentrating on the tasks ahead of her. In the mirror across from the shower stall, she noticed something dark on her stomach. She glanced down in fear, visions of enormous leeches flashing into her brain.

What she saw was less nauseating but even more unbelievable. She turned off the water and stared some more.

Whatever had happened last night? Len Thompson had a hell of a lot of explaining to do.

HE'D BEEN waiting for her to arrive. No way, knowing Janey as he did, would she would let this go without at least railing on his ass a little. Which was good, because once the shouting stopped, they'd be able to get their new situation out in the open as soon as possible.

Didn't mean he was looking forward to the conversation, though.

It had been one hellish night. Having her finally collapse into a restless sleep on his bed had been the only saving grace. Today wasn't looking to be much better, not when it started by having to get his sister to come over. Explaining to Katy what had happened had been bad enough, but with Janey sleeping in so long, showdown at O.K. Corral was going to go down right smack dab in the middle of the family-run Thompson and Sons garage.

Fortunately, by the time Janey jerked opened the door from the back parking lot and rushed in like she owned the place, coffee break had begun. All the guys who worked the shop—Len's three brothers, his dad, and Katy's partner—had vanished into the staff room earlier.

So he was alone to admire the wildcat expression in her eyes. Her hair was pulled back into two pigtails, and for a moment she looked twelve again, not the relentless seductress he'd had to deal with the night before.

He'd expected a bit of an attitude, but the sheer flaming belligerence flashing in her eyes was a surprise.

She stomped across the concrete floor of the garage, jerking to a halt only inches away from him as she stuck a finger in his face. "You've got a shit-ton of explaining to do."

"How're you feeling this morning?" Len folded his arms across his chest, attempting to create a barrier between him and the glaring young woman.

"How the hell am I supposed to feel the night after all sorts of things happened I can't remember? I mean, thank you for taking care of me after that jackass slipped me the drugs—I'm grateful, I really am. Katy told me you looked after me, but there's a whole lot she didn't know about. Am I right?"

She wasn't beating around the bush. "You were a bit of a handful."

"A handful?" Her volume increased, and she planted both fists on her hips. She was much smaller than him, but right then she seemed a towering bundle of fury. "What exactly did I do that made this seem like a good idea?"

She whipped off her T-shirt, and Len's heart leapt into his throat. "*Jeez*, Janey, put your clothes on."

She tucked the hand holding the shirt behind her back, pointing her free fingers like a gun at the printed words on her abdomen.

At least this time she was wearing a bra, which was a whole lot more than she'd had on the last time he had gotten up close and personal with the bold black marks decorating her skin.

"Len Thompson, you tell me right now why your signature is on my belly. Along with what looks like my handwriting saying *Len + Janey 4ever.*"

A distant rumble of voices grew louder, and Len glanced over his shoulder to see the staff room door opening. It was bad enough to have to deal with this, but he couldn't allow anyone to see Janey half-naked in the middle of the family garage.

He turned back and braced himself. "I'll explain everything, but not here."

She shook her head. "I'm not going anywhere without some answers."

Len gave up trying to convince her. Simply leaned over and planted his shoulder against her stomach, grabbed hold of her legs and picked her up. She squawked in dismay, but he ignored her complaining, heading for the exit at a rapid clip. He had them outside and tucked in next to the propane shed in no time, out of sight from anyone who might wander into the garage yard.

"Put me down this instant, you big lughead." Janey punctuated her complaints by smacking her fists into his back.

"We're not discussing anything in front of my family." Len lowered her to the ground, careful she had her balance before letting go. He snatched her T-shirt from her hand and thrust it forward. "Put your clothes on."

Janey folded her arms over her chest, her chin rising defiantly. "Why is your signature on my body?"

"Because it was the only way to get you to stop..." Len paused, not because he wasn't going to tell her the truth, but because there had to be a better way to say this than simply blurting it out.

In front of him, her defiance lessened and her bluster faded. "Damn, what the hell did I try to do to you?"

He couldn't stop the smile that twitched his lips. "Not much more than anything you've tried before."

"Shit." Janey sighed, jerking her shirt over her head. "So. You got to take care of me while I was high, and I basically offered myself to you. Again."

"It wasn't all about sex," Len reassured her. "You ran the gambit. You asked for a hug at one point, and when I gave you one, you started crying."

She frowned, leaning back on the corrugated metal of the shed wall. "Crying?"

"You said I would never hug you unless you were dying. Then we had a long conversation about how you were not dying, and then you got really fascinated with your hands. Which somehow led into a conversation about how your mom would kill you if you ever handed in notes where your handwriting was that crooked."

"Great." She rolled her eyes. "Anything else I should know about?"

Nope. Not telling her, not even if she insisted. Some things he couldn't say out loud without fucking dying all over. "Not really."

She tugged at the bottom of her shirt, exposing a little of the sharpie markings on her belly. One brow shot up again, but she didn't say anything. Just waited, expectantly.

Fine. It seemed this was going to happen, and Len couldn't even feel remorseful about it. "After you'd had a shower—because you insisted you were being consumed by a million, trillion ants, you got a little...affectionate."

Janey's head banged on the shed wall. She closed her eyes and cursed softly. "Fab. What did I do? Try to give you a hickey?"

She honestly looked so upset by the whole situation Len didn't have the heart to tell her all the details. Like how he'd had to go in the shower with her because he was afraid she wouldn't stay vertical. And no way would he show her the scratch marks she'd left on his back. "Don't worry. I wasn't offended."

"But for some reason I decided to do a semipermanent tattoo, and get you to autograph it."

"You were rather insistent."

She shook her head, regaining her feet as she moved away from the wall. "Well, thanks again for taking care of me. And sorry I was a pain in the ass."

She tried to walk around him, but Len shot out his hand and caught her by the elbow. "I'll come by your place around six."

Janey's brows shot skyward. "Hello?"

"For our first date. We can hit the diner for supper." Maybe last night he'd had his arm twisted, but now that he'd wrapped his head around the situation, being together with her was all he could think about.

Being with her was all he'd ever wanted, really.

"Oh, for fuck's sake." Janey shook her arm as if her feeble wiggle could make him let go. "I was out of it, and you pacified me. I get it. Don't jerk my chain."

"I'm not joking." Len shifted forward, backing her toward the shed with his body. "Yes, you were high. But you said a couple things while you were flying that made a lot of sense."

He had her trapped in position. His forearms rested on the shed, leaning in close enough she had to tilt her head to look at him.

"You're serious? You want to take me on a date?"

Len stroked the back of his forefinger up her arm. Teasing gently over the edge of her T-shirt until he could draw his fingers along her collarbone. She was so damn soft. "That's what the writing on your belly says. That you and I are going out. I signed it, and trust me, no matter how wild you were talking, if I hadn't wanted to, I wouldn't have agreed."

Janey shivered under his touch. He rested his hand on her shoulder and was slowly brushing his thumb back and forth along the edge of her neckline. "This is insane, Len. I've tried to get you to go out with me for years. I have done the stupidest things—"

"You don't have to bring them up."

27

She had the cutest little frown creasing her forehead. "But now, after all that time, you and I are dating?"

"Yes."

She snorted. "Bullshit."

"Why? Don't you want to go out with me anymore?" He'd be the one calling bullshit if she said no.

She opened and closed her mouth a few times, seriously struggling to respond. Janey finally shrugged and pulled a face. "It doesn't seem like this is real. Maybe I'm still high." Her gaze narrowed. "Are you sure you're not pulling a fast one on me?"

"Nope." He kept touching her, unable to stop. It was as if now that he'd given himself permission, holding back any longer was impossible.

Her eyes grew wider as he slipped his hand behind her head and cradled her carefully. Temptation lured him forward, calling him to lean down and take her lips for the first time, right there and then.

His body was primed for anything, and everything. Far too hard from simply standing this close—he was going to have a hell of a time surviving when he actually touched her.

Her lashes fluttered, and she stopped fighting. Instead, she planted her palms against his chest, the warmth shooting a thrill through his system. "For real? Because I swear, if I find out you're shitting me, I will peel you like a grape."

Len laughed, the sound coming out shaky as Janey dragged her nails down his chest. "I would like to see you try, but no. I'm serious." He covered her hands with his, mesmerized again by their softness. "This is real, you and me."

Her tongue darted out over her bottom lip, and another shot of fire raced up his spine. Yet somehow, Len pulled away. Setting her free and placing some distance between them in spite of the disappointment on her face.

He knew the sensation. "I'll see you at six."

And he turned, and walked away. Doing his best to hide exactly how difficult it was leave her behind.

Chapter Three

IF SHE'D been confused that morning, her condition hadn't changed much in the past four hours. Janey paused in the middle of her sanding to stare at the wall.

She had a date with Len. That was the last thing she could have imagined.

It was what she wanted, but a sense of unreality hung over the whole situation. While he had finally agreed to go out with her—it still made no sense. Or at least not yet.

One thing for certain, she was going to get to the bottom of the mystery of his change of mind. If not tonight, eventually. Len might not be a huge conversationalist, but she could be a squeaky wheel if she had to.

The contrast between her plans for the night compared to the previous evening struck.

A moment of fear rushed in, and she pushed the sensation out just as quickly. The fact someone had slipped her drugs while in public would make her more cautious in the future, but she refused to allow fear to rule her.

Still, if she ever saw that cowboy again? He'd be riding sidesaddle for the rest of his earthly days.

In the meantime, now that her head no longer ached, she had a long list of things to accomplish in a relatively short time. She turned the sander back on and applied it to the floorboards, working to level the surface.

This was the house she had grown up in, and it was going to help her dreams come true. Not because she thought the structure or location was the best ever, even though she loved the place, but because the house would prove she could stand on her own two feet.

She adjusted the coveralls she wore, the logo on the front a bold red hammer framed with the words "Handy Gal". Around the house, she had three major projects underway, all of which she had to finish before she painted the walls and finished the trim.

But she loved the work. Every dirty, dusty task, no matter how hard it was for her family to understand.

She wasn't interested in getting a line of letters behind her name like the rest of the family. Her mom and dad's decision to move had been the perfect opportunity. She would do a modified flip on the family home. Deal with the needed repairs, plus modernize everything that had been neglected, because considering the rest of the lot of them were a batch of geniuses, the house was rather worn down.

And when she sold the place, it wasn't only the money in the bank she was looking forward to. It was going to the family with her head held high in spite of being the only one with nothing but a high school diploma.

Her hands and brain worked just fine, only down a different track than the rest of them. She was happy with her career choices. Why weren't they?

The sound of the sander buzzed in her ears even after she'd stopped it. Janey laid aside her tools and grabbed the broom to tidy up. She'd barely gotten started when her phone rang.

She examined the screen and fought the urge to make rude faces like a little kid. "Oh joy, oh bliss."

Marty Jons. The bane of her existence. She debated ignoring the call, but that would only increase the chances of her parents calling to check up on her.

"Mr. Jons, how nice." Gack. Janey hated lying, even for social conventions. "What can I help you with?"

The man's patronizing chuckle grated on her nerves like always. "I'm calling to see if I can give *you* a hand with anything. You staying safe over there, young lady?"

"Sure am," Janey quipped back brightly. "Same as yesterday, and the day before that."

He paused, and she felt a little guilty. Was he wondering if that was sarcasm in her voice?

"You know your parents worry about you. I feel it's only right I take the time to reassure them."

Fuck that. She was pretty sure Jons was the reason her parents had any concern in the first place. She swore the man was feeding them updates, and not accurate ones. "Things are going very well with the renovation. Thanks for your concern, but I'm doing very well."

And if she stayed on the phone with him much longer, she'd probably find a way to say *very well* another dozen times.

"Well, if you hit any snags, you be sure to let me know. I've got lots of contacts in the community, and they're all at your disposal."

Lots of contacts? A nephew who swung a hammer, who also did renovations. Janey wondered if Brad was pissed off she was taking business away from him. "I'll definitely keep that in mind. Thanks for touching base."

She had her finger halfway to the end call when his voice carried from the speaker. "Have you given any more thought to my suggestion regarding the apartment?"

The man simply never gave up. Janey could appreciate his determination in some ways—she had a reputation for being a bit of a bulldog herself—but right now? No way would she be the one who caved. "Right in the middle of some thing, can't really talk right now. So good of you to phone. All the best to Mrs. Jons."

She hung up without too much guilt, tucking her phone away and getting back to her task.

But her happiness at the rapidly approaching evening dimmed as her annoyance rose. The only thing stopping her from telling Mr. Jons to take a flying leap was the fact he was good friends with her parents. Telling him to fuck off was tempting, but the sentiment would go over like a sack of bricks.

Hell, he was probably *trying* to get her in trouble.

She couldn't resist one long, loud shout, more a roar of displeasure than any particular word. The sound echoed nicely off the bare walls, ringing in her ears.

"I hope that's not some side effect from what happened to you last night."

Janey whipped around, smiling at her friend who had let herself in the kitchen door. "The screaming? Boy, if that was the only side effect, it would be pretty low on the crazy list."

Shannon placed her purse on the counter before determinedly marching forward to examine Janey. She took control, moving Janey into position to peer into her eyes, clicking her tongue and shaking her head. "You are one of the luckiest fools I have ever met."

"But you do agree I'm lucky, so there's that." Janey wiggled from under Shannon's hands. "I didn't break anything. I don't even have a headache anymore."

"Dehydrated? Seeing stars? Any unusual or erratic behavior I need to watch out for?"

"Does the urge to throw darts at my parents' best friend count, because other than that, situation is pretty normal."

It took less than a second for Shannon to figure out her cryptic comment. "Mr. Jons hounding you again?"

Well. It wasn't her imagination, not when her friends even noticed. "I still haven't figured out his game, but I know it's not from the goodness of his heart that he's checking up on me all the time."

"He sells real estate. You're fixing a house. It's not that strange he's interested in what you're doing." Shannon wandered farther into the living room, looking up at the repairs to the ceiling Janey had already finished. "Maybe he wants to sell the place once you're done."

"Then why doesn't he come out and say that instead of being creepy?" Janey was sure his motives weren't as pure as Shannon suggested. "Plus he keeps going on about that damn apartment he has for rent. I have zero interest in moving into anything he owns."

Shannon shrugged. "Well, you don't have to have anything to do with him if you don't want to. Ignore him."

"The list of people to ignore is getting bigger," Janey complained. If it wasn't Jons, it was one of her older siblings. She stopped in the middle of the room and examined the improvements. "Joe called the other day, wondering if I wanted help filling in college registration forms for the fall."

"Oh, hon. not again."

"And Pamela offered to send me another of those tests. You know the ones, to help you figure out what career you're best suited for." Janey made a face. "You think my brother and sister would have learned by now I'm made of different stock. Maybe not as classy as them, but I like myself."

"You are made of fine stock," Shannon reassured her. "You don't have to go to college or university to make a good living, especially when you find something you like to do."

"Hey, no arguments from me." Janey pointed in the general direction of Calgary where the family had all moved. "But you're going to have to do a hell of a lot more talking to convince my parental units and sibling one and sibling two that what I'm doing is valuable. After all, I'm not saving lives, teaching future generations or discovering a greener source of energy."

"I refuse to respond to that." Shannon folded her arms over her chest. "I know they're your family, but sometimes they are nothing but enormous jackasses."

Janey grinned at Shannon's blunt statement. "I like being Handy Gal. It's never boring, I usually enjoy the job, and I get to make something shiny out of a mess."

"Screw the negative comments. You're good at what you do." Shannon motioned toward the door. "If you really are feeling fine after last night's adventure, you want to come have a bite to eat with me? I just got off shift, and I need to crash in a couple of hours. But if you want to join me for a break, I'm game."

It was tempting, but her deadlines were real. Especially with the other twist in her life. "I shouldn't take off. There's a lot to do, and I have a date tonight."

Her friend smiled. "Getting tossed to the side for a guy. Story of my life. Who's the lucky stiff?"

Janey paused for theatrical effect. "Len."

Shannon's jaw dropped. When she finally snapped her mouth closed, she'd switched her amusement for a frown. "What the hell did you do to him?"

Janey laughed. "Well, that's nice. I tell you I've finally got a date with the guy I've been chasing for years, and you think I did something evil to him?"

"Yes." Shannon dodged under Janey's halfhearted swing. "Come on, admit it. This is the last thing I expect to hear from you after..."

"After you foisted my spaced-out carcass on him last night?" Janey shook a hand before Shannon could protest. "And I'm kidding. I know you had to work, and once I fully woke up this morning, I remembered Liz is off on holidays. I'm *very* grateful nothing bad happened last night." A shiver hit involuntarily, and Shannon laid a hand on her arm. Janey took a deep breath to get her head back into the right place. "Seriously, it's okay, and while I'm not sure exactly what went on, Len insists I didn't blackmail him or anything."

Shannon considered. "It's not that I don't think you'd make a cute couple. It's just you've been interested in him for so long."

For the first time Janey felt a flush of embarrassment. "God, we're only going to hear *that* comment a million more times."

Her friend nodded. "Unfortunately, yes." She paused. "I was going to tease you about watching out for old girlfriends who might spit in your eye, but I don't remember Len going with anyone steady-like."

Janey shook her head. "Never has. Or at least not that I noticed."

"Which means it never happened, because, hon?" Shannon winked. "If you don't know all the details of an event in the man's life, then it never happened."

Shannon left, and Janey settled in to finish fixing the subfloor. The entire time she worked, her brain swirled between images of her perfect brother and sister with their perfect high-paying jobs, and their well-meant but interfering offers. Add in the strange attention from Mr. Jons, and all the unanswered questions she had.

The biggest of which were questions about the man she was officially seeing for the first time tonight.

The idea of calling Katy hit—did she need to warn her best friend? Or would she think the date was some kind of post-drug hallucination? Oh God, what if it was? What if the entire thing had only been in Janey's imagination?

She laughed at herself, and went back to work. One way or another, tonight was going to be an experience.

LEN PULLED up to the curb outside her house, putting the truck in park before taking a deep breath to steady his nerves.

Nerves. *What the hell.* She'd been around forever, and they knew each too well from all the years of Janey and his sister being constantly underfoot.

But the world had changed last night, and Len had to admit it made the coming evening different. The remembered softness to her skin changed things in other ways he wasn't ready to dwell on too hard. Not if he wanted to make it through the date without turning into an absolute fool. Still, his heart was working a whole lot harder than it should have.

He was reaching for his door when a familiar truck approached from the opposite direction. He rolled down his window, coming face-to-face with his oldest brother, Clay. With Janey's house on the shortest route between the shop and Clay's place, it was a natural shortcut home for all of them.

Timing still sucked as far as Len was concerned, although him being outside Janey's wasn't as unusual as it could have been.

Clay frowned. "Did Katy need you to pick something up?" he asked.

Ha. His brother had jumped to the most obvious conclusion. It was only that morning he'd made the date with Janey, and people in his world were about to discover things had changed. There was no use in pretending or trying to keep it a secret. The instant he and Janey walked in the door of the café, news would spread like wildfire.

But then again, Clay was family. They were the ones you were supposed to jerk around.

"I'm picking something up," he admitted.

It was rather amusing when his clue was totally missed. "Are you going back to the garage tonight?" his brother asked.

"No."

Clay made a face. "Damn. We need to switch up the propane cylinders."

"Do it first thing in the morning." Just because Clay had no plans for the evening, didn't mean the rest of them wanted to go back to work. Even if Len didn't have a date, he didn't want to be working all the time, not like Clay seemed determined to do.

Clay paused for a beat. "Fine. But don't let me forget."

"Right."

Len's tone must have given him away, because Clay's expression changed to a full-out glare. "What's that supposed to mean?"

Of all the things he didn't want to start then and there was a conversation about how anal Clay could be about upkeep and safety around the garage. Instead of getting into a drawn-out debate, Len went for his typical peacemaker approach. "You won't forget. You never forget anything important."

The reassurance didn't seem to sink in all the way, but Clay nodded. "Say hi to Katy and Gage when you see them."

They'd both said goodbye to Gage not even an hour ago before he'd left the shop, but Len kept his mouth zipped. "Later."

Clay took off, and Len headed toward the house, considering perhaps this was another good reason for making changes in his life. Since his mom had died, he and his family had grown close. Maybe too close. It wasn't that he didn't want to spend time with them, but living in each other's pockets got stupid occasionally.

Combine a close-knit family with small-town social habits, and Len was on the verge of becoming a hermit in self-defense.

There were things he didn't want in his life, but being absolutely alone was no longer what he aspired to. He was very determined the people in his life would be the people he chose, no matter how much willpower that took.

And it seemed Janey was at least temporarily on his chosen list. *Finally.*

He closed the distance to her front door with a lot more enthusiasm than even five minutes ago, eager to get things rolling.

A small yellow sticky note was taped to the inside of the window.

Renovations underway. Please use back entrance.

Len caught himself smiling as he walked to the back door. He hadn't spent a lot of time at the Watsons' house, but the place was familiar enough from the times he'd come to grab Katy to bring her home.

Mr. and Mrs. Watson had always come and spoken with him, politely inquiring about his parents, and later, once his mom had passed away, asking about his father and his brothers. He didn't remember much about

41

Janey's siblings. They were a fair bit older and had gone away to university as soon as they finished high school.

He'd met the Watsons dozens of times, and to this day he still wasn't sure if they had come to the door to make him feel comfortable, or to do the exact opposite. It wasn't so much what they said, but how they said it. Always so formal. He certainly hadn't been in any rush to get close with the family.

Len stepped up on the porch and pushed the bell. Inside the house a musical doorbell played a fancy tune that echoed through the open screen door.

"Hang on, I'm almost ready."

Something in the distance fell with a rolling crash, and Len shuffled his feet, his amusement rising. Janey, in contrast to her parents, had never been anywhere near what he'd call formal. Maybe he wasn't the only one feeling the tension.

He stared through the glass, hauling in every bit of patience he had as a momentary glimpse of leg flashed past at the end of the hall. His body reacted far too eagerly, and Len deliberately looked toward the ground, steadying his breathing.

"You don't have to stand outside," Janey called. "The door is unlocked. Come in and grab a drink, if you want."

He took the bull by the horns and stepped through the entrance. That was about as far as he'd ever gotten before, so he slipped off his shoes and moved cautiously into the kitchen.

The walls were patched in places, small scraps of old tile and wallpaper visible in the bin by the door. Janey was going to town on her renovations, and he liked what he saw. She wasn't only changing paint colour and surface trim. She was fixing things from the inside out, and he wasn't at all surprised.

If anyone would do a hundred percent thorough job, it would be Janey.

He kept going until he hit the living room, checking out the new hardwood underfoot. Home improvements weren't his thing. He preferred to play around in the innards of an engine, but he could appreciate what he was seeing around the place.

And then he twisted, and all thoughts about household renovations vanished as he spotted Janey.

Considering how petite she was, her legs shouldn't look as if they went on forever. Yet somehow that's the impression he got at the long length revealed by the teeny skirt she'd pulled on. The fabric clung to her hips, partnered with a short-sleeved T-shirt, both jet black and skintight. Instead of pulling her hair into her usual ponytail, the mass was all bundled up at the back of her head, magically held in place as far as he could tell. A couple strands hung loosely on either side of her face, and as she walked toward him, her smile was perfectly framed. She held a sweater in her hands, a brilliant blue colour that made him think of clear winter days.

He was so busy admiring her he forgot to say anything.

The next thing he knew she was staring up, her sweet smile shifting toward mischief. "Hey."

"Hey, yourself." He helped her slip into her sweater. It was just an excuse to touch her, and he damn well knew it.

"I hope this is okay. It's finally warm enough to wear a skirt, and I've been dying to wear this one." She took a couple steps away from him, leaning over to grab a pair of low heel shoes from the dining room floor.

Len's gaze dropped over her hips and legs. "I don't mind."

He didn't mind at all, only the control he had wrestled back a few moments earlier was utterly gone. Good thing his jeans were slightly loose, because he needed every damn inch of space.

Janey finished adjusting the straps over the back of her heels, mesmerizing him with every move. She straightened then tilted her head toward the door. "I'm starving. How about you?"

He had her outside and into his truck in no time flat. Helping her up into the high seat in spite of her denial.

"I am capable of using a runner board," she teased.

He paused in the doorframe, hanging on to the truck frame and admiring her legs as she twisted on the bench seat. "Humour me."

As he got behind the steering wheel, the temptation was there to order her into the center seat. Fortunately, she read his mind, shuffling over and doing up her seatbelt without him saying a word.

Her thigh pressed against his, and warmth seeped through his jeans. Somehow he focused on the road ahead of them, and drove the short distance to the café parking lot.

They were through the front door before he had time to talk himself out of it. All eyes turned toward them, the same as always when people came in. But this time, instead of going back to their dinners, at least half kept staring.

He and Janey had been seen together often enough doing things for Katy, some of them probably figured that's all this was. But the more alert townsfolk? They sensed something was different.

One of the waitresses slid forward, the ready smile she always had for him flashing bright. "Good to see you guys. You grabbing takeout for Katy and Gage?"

Janey cleared her throat. Len figured the strange noise was her hiding her amusement.

And not answering the question. She flicked her gaze to meet his, and laughter shone in the depths.

It was up to him. A dare? "Nope. We're eating in."

Tessa's eyes widened. "You're what?"

He should have known this was coming. Tessa had tried to date him before, and it had taken a lot of effort on his part to turn her down without hurting her feelings. Now? He bet her curiosity would be on high, and the inquisition would start.

"Any open booths by the window?" Janey asked before Tessa could find her voice to comment.

The waitress blinked. "Of course. Right this way."

She led them past three or four open tables, weaving through the room to reach the exact center of the café.

Len figured she'd done it on purpose. Like putting them on parade.

Tessa gestured to the table. "Here you go. And here are your menus. The specials are on the board."

She sped away without announcing them like she usually would, darting behind the counter and vanishing into the kitchen.

Janey slipped onto the bench seat, soft laughter rising from her lips. "Tessa doesn't want to miss out being the bearer of bad news to all your hopeful love interests."

Len sat next to her, making Janey slide over toward the wall instead of taking the seat opposite her. "Whatever turns her on."

Their legs were touching, and he could smell the scent of her shampoo, but the torment of being that close was better than sitting across from her and having to make eye contact.

Or worse, having to keep his eyes from eating her up.

It was right, being there with her. Didn't mean this relationship was going to be easy, but then again...

That was one lesson he'd learned a long time ago—

The right thing to do was rarely easy.

Chapter Four

JANEY PLAYED with the edge of the menu as she nonchalantly glanced around the room. They were still the topic of conversation for a lot of the evening diners, but she could handle that.

It wasn't as if she hadn't dated before. She knew the rules. Everyone in Rocky Mountain House seemed to know everything about...well, *everything*. A lack of privacy was a fact of small-town living, and attempting to keep secrets was a waste of time, especially when there was no reason for anything to be secret.

Ignoring curious glances was second nature by now, especially for the girl who had been the black sheep in her family. Not because she was *bad*, but she had never been as smart, as sophisticated, or as charismatic as the rest of them.

As long as she got to enjoy life, she really didn't mind.

Right now it was more important to take full advantage of the first time in forever she'd been alone with Len Thompson. Time to do something other than chase him. She'd rarely gotten to simply sit and talk without others being a part of the conversation.

The idea of being alone with him for more intimate reasons was also on her agenda, but she hadn't been *solely* fixated on his body these past years, as fine as that body was. Still, she had healthy admiration for the set of biceps accidentally caressing her arm every time he moved. He'd pulled off his jacket and hung it on the rail beside the table, and now there was nothing covering him but that faded T-shirt mercilessly stretched over curved musculature. She couldn't wait to explore more thoroughly.

But exploring was for dessert.

"Did you ever finish the overhaul on that classic truck?" she asked.

He jumped on the topic. "Not yet. I'm waiting for a couple of parts, but I hope to have her roadworthy by the end of summer."

"Are you going to get her painted?"

He nodded, flipping through the menu even though he had to have it memorized by now. "Still deciding what colour."

"Candy-apple red, of course."

Len shook his head. "Too flashy."

She paused, and thought it through. He was right. That was a colour she'd go for. Something that would stand out on the road and make an impression. Len liked to fade into the background more.

"She'd look good in midnight black, but that's not a great colour for driving around on dusty back roads. You'd spend more time washing her than driving her."

Len leaned an elbow on the table and twisted to face her. His other arm stretched along the top of the backrest, warmth seeping toward her. Having his full concentration focused her direction made a spark of heat flutter through her body. "True."

"Gray or white you wouldn't have to wash so often." Janey made a face. "But I don't think a paint that bland would cut it. They would make your beautiful truck look like an albino June bug."

Across from them, someone slid onto the bench seat, and they both turned in surprise to discover his younger brother staring innocently at them.

"You guys waiting for a pickup?" Troy went on without waiting for their answer. "I'm grabbing lasagna for me and Dad. I'll wait with you."

Janey stifled her amusement, tempted to nudge Len with her shoulder.

"Go away," Len ordered.

Troy leaned back, pulling out his phone and staring at the screen. "Forget it, bro. We're off the pay-clock, and you don't boss me around out here."

Len stiffened. Janey laid a hand on his thigh. Maybe if she tried the message would sink in. "Troy, go away," she said sternly.

That was enough to help him realize something was off. He tore his gaze off his phone and glanced back and forth between the two of them, his eyes widening as he put two and two together. "Shit. You aren't waiting for an order, are you?"

Janey blinked. Len didn't say anything.

And then the bastard had the gall to just sit there and grin. "Well, this is a surprise."

"What part of 'go away' did you not understand?" Len demanded.

"So, what can I get for you guys tonight?" Tessa was back, her notepad in hand as she eyed everyone at the table, no doubt eager for gossip.

Janey was fighting a serious case of the giggles. "Burger and fries, strawberry milkshake. Thanks, Tessa."

"Double bacon cheeseburger," Len said, "and don't bother asking my brother what he wants. He's going to the counter to order."

"Oh, I don't mind staying here," Troy offered. He checked out Tessa, his dark eyes flashing as he admired her. "You're looking good tonight."

"You too, Troy." She returned his smile, but she was still more interested in the whole Len-and-Janey show. She hesitated, examining both the brothers for a moment before finally breaking down and asking, "Where am I taking your order? Here or at the counter?"

"At the counter," Len and Janey said simultaneously.

Troy's grin stretched from ear to ear. "No problem. Catch you two later."

He slipped off the bench and past Tessa, who paused for just long enough to confirm she'd bring out their orders once they were ready.

Silence fell over the table for all of ten seconds before Janey couldn't hold back any longer. She laughed, trying to keep the sound soft enough the neighbouring tables wouldn't be aware.

Beside her, Len wasn't nearly as tense anymore. He snuck his hand over hers and linked their fingers together, and suddenly the temperature in the room rose.

"This is going to be very entertaining," Janey whispered, not completely sure which part she was referring to—their dinner out, or the subtle sexual tension twisting up her arm as he moved his thumb slowly back and forth over her skin.

He made a noise, somewhere between a snort and a grunt, which only set her off again. This time she couldn't keep her volume down, and her outright laugh drew the attention of people who had gone back to their meals.

"Next time I'm cooking for you, instead of going through this circus," Len warned.

She waved her free hand in the air. "They'll get bored of it, eventually."

But the entire time they sat there, it seemed they were the best entertainment in town. One after another Janey's or Len's friends who happened into the café all slid into that empty space across from them. Made small talk for a moment or two before their jaws hit the table as they realized they were interrupting a *date*.

By the fourth time it happened even Len snickered out loud.

"We should start charging by the minute," Janey suggested.

Len shook his head. "I knew they were a lot of busybodies, but what is so entertaining about us?"

Janey snuck a french fry off his plate. "That's probably my fault."

This time his laugh was lower, more intimate. "Okay."

She leaned her shoulder against him, feeling warm from her head to her toes. "You're supposed to take the blame. Don't you know the rules?"

It was like a light switch flipped. All his lighthearted amusement vanished between one breath and the next, and Len went from teasing and warm to tense. Every inch of him on alert.

"What's wrong?" she asked quietly.

"Nothing." He focused on his plate, finishing the rest of his meal in silence. The quiet camaraderie they'd shared vanished as if it had never been.

Janey poked a fry into her ketchup and ate it slowly, considering what exactly had gone wrong. She wasn't going to push, not here in such a public place, but if she and Len were going to be a couple?

His days of being Mr. Silent, at least with her, were coming to an end.

LEN STARED out the front window and held on tight to the steering wheel. Seated next to him, Janey was telling him about what she had coming in for completing the trim around the house. It was easy enough to listen and make appropriate noises, and still use most of his brain to give himself a good solid lecture.

Less than an hour into officially dating her, and he'd already acted like a jackass. And over such a stupid thing, because there was no way she could know her words would trigger a flood of memories.

He and guilt went way back. Guilt, and a whole ton of fear as well.

It seemed that was the way his screwed-up insecurities worked these days, coming out to smack him out of the blue. For the most part he had made his peace with what had happened so many years ago, then he'd be blindsided and all over it was like being pushed into a dark pit.

The strangest things could set him off. A combination of words, the scent of antiseptic like at the hospital.

One time someone's phone had gone off, and their ring tone had been a series of beeps eerily reminiscent of a heart-rate monitor. He'd come within three seconds of snatching the phone right out of their hands and grinding the case to pieces under his heel.

But whatever took him there, he'd suddenly be fifteen again, watching his family fall apart around him as his mother fought a battle she couldn't win.

A soft touch landed on his arm as Janey leaned her head against his shoulder. She'd gone silent. He'd probably missed responding to some bit of conversation for longer than was polite.

"I'm sorry. I'm being a shit."

She'd curled up, legs on the seat as she wrapped her fingers around his right biceps. "You looked as if you're thinking deep thoughts. I'm okay with that. Not everyone is as obsessed about wood-staining methods as I am."

That hauled a chuckle from him. "It really is hard to not end up smiling when you're around."

Janey twisted in her seat, leaning forward far enough she was in his line of vision without taking his eyes off the road. "I think that's one of the nicest things anyone has ever said to me."

"It's true."

She loosened off her seatbelt so she could stay there, resting her elbow on the dashboard as she smiled back. "I hope this is another fact that makes you smile even if it's a little embarrassing. Did you know that you're driving in circles?"

Len glanced out the window. "Damn."

She laughed. "Whatever is on your mind has you all tangled up. Push it aside for a little while, and let's go have some fun."

He wasn't sure he was up for hitting the dance floor or anything like that. "You want to go somewhere else tonight?"

She tilted her head from side to side. "I've had enough of being the center ring at the circus. I was thinking more somewhere to stretch our legs."

"The trail? Down by the river?"

"I don't want to go back by the river yet." Janey made a face. "I made a bit of a fool of myself the last time."

Another thing he should've thought of sooner. "How're you feeling? Any lingering aftereffects?"

"God, I hope not." She pointed ahead of them toward the turnoff for the wilderness park. "Of course, you must be twice as happy that I'm not acting up, so you don't have to babysit me tonight."

"Well, not all of it was bad." Len slipped a hand off the wheel and rested it on her thigh. "Trust me, I enjoyed it when you started taking off your clothes."

The low growl that escaped her just made him grin harder.

"Are you really going to taunt me about that?" she asked.

"Hell, yeah." He glanced over. Her lips were thrust forward in a slight pout, but amusement danced in her dark eyes, along with a healthy dose of lust. He took the corner a little too fast, and she swayed, soft curves connecting with his arm before he caught hold around her waist and pinned her in place.

"I want to make some memories I can look back on," Janey murmured. "Right now you're the only one who's sure what I did last night."

"And you're the only one I will ever tease about it." He put the truck in park, turning off the ignition to give her his full concentration. "I kinda like having something to tease you about, but what happened last night is between us. I promise that's as far as it will ever go."

Janey sat for a moment, staring seriously before nodding.

Anticipation rose between them. He was still holding her waist, his hand resting on bare skin. So soft and warm, he could hardly wait to explore.

And her lips—she'd just licked them. Her tongue had darted over the full bottom swell and left it wet. Every bit of him was ready to finally get to satisfy his cravings. *She* was the one he'd wanted for so long. The only one.

She tilted her chin and glanced at him from under her lashes. "Want to go for a walk?"

Janey was across the bench seat and out the door before he could respond one way or another. He took a deep breath and hit the ground, adjusting himself as discreetly as he could under the guise of closing his door.

She met him at the front of the truck, her hand held out. He slipped her fingers into his, amazed how the electric shock of anticipation turned his entire system alive.

"You have anything big happening at the garage in the next while?" she asked.

"Typical maintenance and summertime vacationers. Nothing too exciting." All his attention was on the connection between them. She had strong hands, probably from swinging a hammer and all the other tools she used on a regular basis. But while she had calluses, she'd done her nails, and she must use cream or something because she was still a lot softer than him.

Jeez. He was holding her fucking hand and ready to write poetry about it.

They strolled along the trail for a good hour, talking easily like people who had known each other for a long time. Well, Janey talked. Len listened, slipping in the occasional word or comment, which was more than usual.

But it was comfortable, and a sense of peace he'd been lacking for a long time grew stronger.

Although, on another level, the tension between them was real. They might've been walking side-by-side, but he still could see and admire everything about her. The mesmerizing curves he'd gotten up close and personal with only the night before. He'd felt her body pressed against his. There'd been a layer of clothing between them, his, but the memory was enough to make him want to hurry his step. To get to the end of the loop and back to the truck, so he could take her home and see what happened next.

Except...

He was drawing a line tonight. Just because they were finally going out, it didn't give him the right to simply take her home and give into the lust raging through him.

He glanced over, and Janey winked, slipping her hand from his to pace backwards down the path in front of him. She wiggled her hips a little harder, and leaned over, the curves of her breasts swaying slightly as she moved.

Dark hair hung low enough the ends of her hair would have just touched the pale red nipples he'd admired the night before.

"You keep looking at me like that," she teased, "and I'm going to spontaneously ignite."

"You're looking mighty fine. I'd hate to see you go up in flames."

She pulled to a stop, and he stepped close enough she had to tilt her head back to stare at him. "I don't know. Little bit of burning could be fun."

Janey pressed her palms to his abdomen, slowly sliding upward until she reached his neck.

Len imitated her in terms of catching hold around her waist, and this time when he tugged her against him, they both let out enormous sighs.

Her smile increased. "I've been looking forward to this forever."

"Not nearly as long as I have," he confessed.

He kept one hand planted firmly in the center of her back. The other he used to cradle the back of her neck, controlling her and angling her the way he wanted as he leaned forward. Slowly. Ever so slowly.

Warmth brushed past his cheek as her breathing increased in tempo. The rock-solid length of his arousal was pressed to her body, and she shifted her hips slightly. Enough that he couldn't stop a groan from escaping.

Their mouths so close, but not yet touching.

Her gaze dropped from his eyes to his lips. "What're you waiting for?" she whispered.

He wanted to say something—hell, he wasn't sure what. Something borderline romantic, maybe.

Only when her tongue darted out there was no way to convince his brain to wait any longer. He closed the distance between their mouths, pressing their lips together. Lightly. Once.

Then again.

She eased open her lips, so he did the same, and the taste of her shot through him, setting off warning bells. It was every bit as good as he'd hoped for, and far, *far* more enticing.

Their bodies were locked together as he took her mouth and controlled her. Kissed her as if this would be the only chance he had, and he needed her in his system to survive.

He hadn't lied. He had wanted this forever, and holding back had taken considerably more strength than he'd ever imagined. Now he took every bit of the restrained longings, and the waiting, and used them to experience her as fully as possible.

It wasn't enough to kiss her. He kissed her lips. He kissed her cheek. He planted a row of kisses along her jawline until he reached a spot underneath her ear that sent her squirming against him. If it was possible, he grew harder, his cock aching for release.

Still wasn't enough. Janey moaned as he put his teeth to her earlobe and nibbled. Changed tactics to trace the tender surface with his tongue. He was rewarded with a full-body shiver that sent him twirling toward the edge.

"Oh, Len. Yes, I like that." She dug her fingers into his shoulders, clutching the fabric of his shirt as she tried to get closer.

He couldn't resist going back to her lips. To the tease of her tongue against his. But with every rub between them, danger approached rapidly.

And when she snuck a hand down his body, circling over his chest and tweaking one of his nipples before crossing his abdomen to tug his shirt free from his jeans, Len knew he wouldn't survive. Not if they continued for a second longer.

He caught hold of her hand. "Not here. Stop, Janey."

The sound of utter devastation escaped her throat. "I'm ready for more," she complained.

He was ready to do that spontaneous-combustion thing she had talked about earlier. "Not here," he insisted.

She took a deep breath then, thank God, eased off her death grip enough he could put some space between their bodies before he had an accident.

"Take me home?" Her words came out husky and low.

Len swallowed hard. "Yes."

She'd obviously forgiven him for being a bonehead in the restaurant. By the time he'd gotten her home, he'd recovered some of his missing brain. He caught hold of her hand as they walked to the back door, bracing himself for the coming storm.

Before disaster struck, he was going to enjoy kissing her all over.

He waited until she'd used her key before twirling her between him and the side of the house. The porch light was still off, but the stars were out, and the moon and the streetlights gave enough light to send shadows dancing everywhere in the yard. Silent witness as he picked her up and pressed her against the wall with his body.

Damn him for being a sick bastard and punishing both of them like this, but he simply couldn't resist feeling her heat once more. She wrapped her legs around him and smiled.

He took her lips, and this time there was not only the newness of the connection, but a touch of familiarity that only made it better.

They kissed until they were both breathless and he was one second away from exploding. He tugged his lips from hers, and they stared into each other's eyes. Her pupils were huge dark moons against the golden brown irises.

"I'll see you tomorrow."

Her expression changed to complete shock as he carefully lowered her to the ground.

"Len?"

He didn't trust himself to speak, so he turned and took the stairs off the porch as quickly as possible, two at a time, afraid if he hesitated he'd reconsider.

"Len." This time her voice was a lot louder and a lot more demanding.

He tossed her a wave. "Give me a call tomorrow. I'm free all day."

He hightailed it back to his truck as fast as he could as all sorts of excuses why he should turn around filled his head.

Chapter Five

NO ONE could torture you like family.

"I swear if he starts singing that kid's song one more time, I'm going to rip his head off," Len threatened. "I don't give a shit who's sitting in what tree—unless it's to toss a rope over a limb and hang Troy high."

His youngest brother grinned, but this time it appeared Len had some backup.

Mitch stepped away from the welding bench. The tattooed flames on his hands and arms rippled as he cracked his knuckles and gave Troy the evil eye. "I'll cut him into small pieces so it's easier to hide the body."

"You two have no sense of humour," Troy complained.

"Or maybe the problem is you couldn't carry a tune in a bucket." Mitch retorted. He twisted towards where Clay and their dad, Keith, were pulling a diagnostic. "Can we send him out for coffee or something?"

"He's just teasing your brother about his new girlfriend. It's not as if you weren't doing the same thing three minutes ago," their dad shouted back.

"But Mitch's joke was funny," Clay offered. "Troy hasn't mastered the art of the insult yet."

"He's still wet behind the ears. He'll learn eventually," Mitch grinned evilly, ducking around the tire station to get away from Troy.

The only one in the room who wasn't family paused in the middle of his tune-up. Or more exactly, Len had to correct himself, the only one in the room who wasn't family by blood. Gage Jenick had joined the family in a decisive way over the past year, and while the wedding still had to take place, he and the youngest of the Thompson family, Katy, were not only rock-solid, they were the parents of the cutest little baby Len had ever seen.

He didn't mind being Uncle Len one bit. As long as he got to give the kids back when they got stinky or started to make noise, his siblings could crank out all the rug-rats they wanted.

His usual mode of staying silent was working in his favour even as the conversation once again narrowed in on him and Janey's change of relationship.

"What I want to know," Gage said, "is why now?"

Len shrugged.

"Oh, come on. The girl has been around forever. And she's been chasing you forever." Mitch agreed with Gage. "Did you just now figure out what to do with your dick—?"

Their dad swatted Mitch on the shoulder as he walked past. "If you're going to take the conversation in that direction, I'll be the one who goes to get coffee."

Good-natured chuckling accompanied his words, though. No way the man could've survived raising five kids through puberty on his own without having had some extraordinarily blunt conversations.

Keith Thompson wasn't the type to beat around the bush and keep it all hush-hush. In fact, Len's earliest memories about getting *the talk* pretty much matched everyone in the room.

Clay confirmed it by bringing the topic up on his own.

"I'm not about to talk about my sex life in front of you, but you really going to pretend like we don't know what goes where?" Clay chuckled. "I think the first time I asked you a question you deliberately called me, Mitch and Len, and sat us down in a row. And the details flew."

Keith paused with his shoulders to the exterior door, the lines around his eyes crinkling as he smiled back at his boys. "No use in doing that job more times than I had to."

"Yeah, maybe. But you know that day? When I asked *where did I come from*?" Clay folded his arms across his chest, the move making his shoulders look even wider, showcasing the resemblance between him and his father, and all the siblings in the room.

"Yeah?"

Clay chuckled lightly. "Daniel Coleman told me he'd been born at home, and someone else at school said they were born in this big hospital in Calgary. That's all I was wondering about. Imagine my shock when instead of telling me which hospital you'd taken Mom to, you started talking about erections and safe sex."

A collective howl went up from the lot of them as their father gave his oldest son an admonishing finger wave then pushed open the door and vanished outside.

The amusement continued for a while, dirt talk and stories ringing out between working on jobs and taking turns to respond to the new customers coming to the front desk. A brief respite from the teasing Len knew would soon be back.

Sure enough, during the next lull, Gage closed in on him. "You know you have to tell me some details about what's going on, because otherwise Katy will never get off my back."

"My little sister can interrogate her friend by herself."

"Not the same." Gage grinned. "Of course, I'll also get to hear about all of your downfalls over the next while, so please make sure you don't screw up too badly. But if I had some juicy tidbits to share with Katy the next time she's pissed off at the entire male species, that would ease my way."

"Spill the beans for the good of mankind," Clay teased. "Or if not for that reason, do it because I'm curious as all hell. You and Janey." He shook his head.

Len paused. "You don't think I should be dating her?"

More than one of the guys responded with a rude noise, only Clay was the one who answered. "I think you should've started dating her years ago. The last I heard, when she finishes the renovation she's planning on rejoining her family in Calgary. You haven't given yourself much time to make this work."

"Make what work?" Troy asked. "He's dating her. They'll fool around a little and have a good time. There's nothing saying it's supposed to be a forever thing."

Strangely, it was Mitch who interrupted. His brother with the who-gives-a-fuck attitude who was now engaged to a cop, of all people. "Don't be so down on the forever shit. It's kind of an awesome feeling."

They'd all gathered in a circle, work tasks forgotten. Len figured this was part of the experience. Getting his brothers on board would only make it easier down the road when Janey left.

Mitch was right, *and* he was totally wrong. What Len wanted was forever. It's what he had *always* wanted with Janey, and what he'd worked so hard to avoid stepping into. Since he knew he couldn't give the woman everything she deserved, he'd refused to give her anything.

Her leaving...changed things.

Maybe he was being selfish, to take for a little while, but he was human. Janey wanted it, and he was too weak to say no to a temporary touch of heaven.

So he turned to Troy instead and acted the ass. "Exactly. Doesn't have to be forever, but it's gonna be a hell of a good time while it lasts."

Clay's eyes narrowed.

Len put up a hand before he could say anything. "Don't."

Again, it was Mitch and Gage who backed him up, the two of the lot who Len figured would have the most problems with him and Janey being a temporary thing.

"Let Len alone," Mitch ordered. "This is between them."

"Except for the usual caveats that if he hurts her I will be obliged to hurt him, because Katy will expect me to." Gage was almost apologetic, but Len understood.

The last thing he intended was to hurt Janey. Hell, that was the whole reason he'd avoided getting together with her in the first place. That was why every night for the past week he'd left her at the door with a kiss and nothing more.

Actually, he was the one in danger of getting hurt. He kind of thought he'd seen her eyeing the hammer and nails the last time he'd been in her house.

The buzzer by the main door went off as someone stepped from the office into the working garage. The lot of them twisted to see who it was, and laughter hit instantaneously.

Janey plopped her fists on her hips and stared them down, her gaze narrowing. "Gee. I wonder who you were talking about?"

She stuck out her tongue before bounding across the floor in a direct path for Len.

"Good luck," Gage whispered before he drifted away.

Len would need more than luck to survive much more anticipation.

Janey's smile grew with each step as the rest of his brothers rushed back to their tasks. "What a sensation of power," she teased. "I'd hate to actually catch you up to no good, and see how fast you move then."

Len didn't pause to think about it. He caught hold of her belt, tugging her close to kiss her. Maybe that's all they were doing yet—kissing—but hell if he wanted to miss any opportunity.

Like always she cuddled against him willingly as he took her lips, all soft and warm and eager, and far too...*inspiring*, considering he had another three hours of work still to go.

It was also far too much of a public display of affection for his family as wolf whistles broke loose from all quadrants of the garage.

Janey stepped away from him, both hands shooting into the air with middle fingers raised high. But she smiled good-naturedly.

"What can I do for you?" Len asked.

"You so sure I need something? What if I came to get today's quota of kisses?" she teased.

He leaned against a workbench, his legs on either side of hers as he kept her close. "If that's the case, cover your ears and pucker up."

Janey laughed as she pressed a hand to his chest. "Actually, I do need something. One of you has your welder's ticket, right? How about gas-fitting?"

Len nodded. "Gage has his A card, and I've got apprentice papers. You have something that needs welding?"

She nodded. "I know how to do it, but this is one of those 'more than a repair job'. I'll need someone to pull a permit for me, as well."

That didn't sound too complicated. "I don't mind helping you. You want to show me what you're doing?"

"Would you?" She glanced around the garage. "I don't want to drag you away from work, but I need it done sooner than later. I can't finish the final installation on the kitchen cupboards until this is out of the way."

Len straightened, enjoying the brief moment of their bodies brushing together. "No problem. Let me tell Clay I'll be gone for the afternoon."

She hesitated. "I didn't mean for you to drop everything on a moment's notice. It can wait until tonight."

"Not a problem," Len insisted. He lowered his volume and gave her a wink. "I have no objections to cutting out of work early, especially if it means I get to spend some time with you."

Her face lit up. "Meet you at the house?"

He nodded. "Let me get the gear in the back of my truck, and I should be there within fifteen."

It was more like thirty before he had finished the one task Clay needed completed, but then his big brother surprised him and let him go without too much teasing.

The job itself took only a little time. Janey had arranged all of the prep work, and done it well.

Len hesitated before turning the equipment on. Instead of handling it himself, he held out the torch. "Why don't you do it? I'll supervise."

He'd guessed right. Her eyes got brighter as she reached for her safety goggles and got herself into position, sturdy leather gloves protecting her hands as she turned on the torch and made quick work of the connection.

She'd have no problems getting this passed during an inspection. "Nice job."

Janey finished putting the torch away, laying her safety gear aside before rejoining him. "It's not my favourite task, but I don't mind it every now and then."

"You did great, and I'll make sure Gage gets you the paperwork."

Then she was no longer all the way across the room from him, but into his personal space, smiling up suggestively. "I should give you a proper thank-you."

Warning signals went off. "You don't have to."

Her smile faded. She paused for a beat, but it was obvious she wasn't going to let the topic go. "Len. Is there a reason why you're avoiding me?"

"I'm not avoiding you." Not in the strictest sense, he wasn't.

One of her brows rose slightly. "You did say we were boyfriend and girlfriend, correct?"

He nodded.

Janey hesitated for the longest time before finally spitting it out. "Okay, when I call us that, it kind of sounds like we're back in fifth grade, which if we were in fifth grade? The fact we've done nothing but kiss would totally make sense."

She'd rested her hands lightly on his chest. Her lips were pulled into the familiar *almost pout*, and he wondered if she knew exactly how much that got to him.

"I just don't see a reason to rush into anything."

Her response was instant amusement. "Oh, Len. It's not rushing for us to do more than kiss."

Her palms moved over his chest, and he caught hold of her waist to keep her tight to his body. His erection had to be very obvious between them.

"In one way, I'm damn impressed," she admitted. "I kind of thought we'd end up in bed that first night."

Len swallowed hard, images flooding his brain.

Janey continued, her hands skimming around the back of his body, sneaking under his shirt until her palms were pressed to his bare skin. "But now I'm wondering if there's a problem."

"What kind of problem?" Len asked, the words improbably low and barely coherent as he fought for control.

"Do you not find me attractive?"

"Jeez, Janey." He caught her around the waist and lifted her on the counter, stepping between her legs and moving until their torsos were connected. Every possible inch pressed tight together. "Trust me, it's not that at all."

"So you say, but…" She shrugged.

He grabbed her hand and pressed it against the raging erection attempting to escape from his jeans. "Does that feel like I'm not attracted to you?"

It was an exquisite torture to allow her fingers to drift freely over him.

"Then why aren't we doing more than kissing?" she asked. "Honest, Len. You don't have to hold back for my sake. It's not like I'm a virgin, or anything."

He couldn't stop the tension from flooding in. The worst thing was she picked up on it, catching hold of his face and forcing him to turn until their eyes met. She had the cutest little frown as she attempted to puzzle it out.

Hell if he was going to help her by actually saying the words.

Her gaze narrowed. "Len. Is there something...?" She bit into her bottom lip momentarily before taking a deep breath and barreling forward. "Tell me I'm insane, but either you are extraordinarily shy, which you have nothing to be worried about, my fine man. Or, you're a..."

Dammit. At this point he *wanted* her to say it.

Because if she did, he wouldn't have to.

"Yes," he forced out.

Confusion hit. "Yes, you're shy. Or yes, you've never had sex?"

He never thought about that. "Both."

A brief flash of disbelief shot over her face along with bewilderment. He was pretty sure she trusted him not to be lying about something this big, but she was still staring as if he had three heads.

"Really? *Really?*"

He let out a massive sigh. "Why is that so hard to believe?"

"Because at least a half dozen women in town all confessed to me at one point or another that they'd slept with you."

Good grief. "You know better than to believe small-town rumor."

She nodded, slightly distracted. "I should've known they were trying to jerk me around. And yet that makes no sense."

"That I've never had sex?"

"Yes!"

"Sorry. It's true." He reached up to play with her hair. If they had to have this conversation at least he could enjoy touching her at the same time.

"It doesn't make sense that you're a virgin," she insisted.

"You're starting to piss me off," Len warned. "It just is. Why is that so hard to believe?"

She snorted. "Because you're a guy."

"Right, so I'm supposed to be happy to stick my dick anywhere just because I'm a guy?"

She snapped her mouth closed and hesitated for long enough to think about her response, which he appreciated, all things considered.

"Okay, so it's totally sexist and totally wrong, but—yeah. That's exactly what most people would assume."

"Bullshit. Maybe some guys are more particular about where we stick our dicks than others."

She still looked unconvinced and completely perplexed. "Just..." She shook her head. "Okay, this makes me a total asshole, but *really?*"

"You say that again, and I'll make you regret it."

"I'm not trying to be rude. I'm flat-out surprised. I mean, does that mean you've never—"

Her question cut off abruptly as her eyes widened and her cheeks flushed red.

Len knew exactly where her mind had gone. He would have laughed, only the moment was too full of sexual expectations to be something to joke about. "I've never—*what?* You're wondering if I've never even jerked off? Trust me, the equipment works just fine."

IT WAS impossible to stop images from flashing into her brain. Len's fingers wrapped around his cock. Long slow strokes following as he worked his shaft, his abdominal muscles growing tighter until he hit the moment of release. Janey couldn't wait to see it in real life.

Maybe they weren't the words she should have spoken, but they were real, and honest, and they burst free before she could stop them.

"Show me."

"*Jeez*, Janey..."

She should have felt shame at her breathless demand, but all that remained was rising heat between her legs and the nearly violent urge to rub one off herself.

"I can help you. Or we can do it at the same time. That's still together."

His eyes grew dark, and his breathing increased in tempo.

She lifted her chin, meeting his gaze. Let him see the desire she felt. "I'm not saying your virginity is something special we should save."

He snorted.

There was no way to stop smiling, even with desire dancing through her veins. "But we don't have to rush into anything. You must've had a reason why you waited, and it's up to you when you tell me why, or if you even *want* to tell me why. But I've honestly wanted more than kisses from you for such a long time. So unless you don't want to do this, let me make you feel good. Or let me watch. Whatever you feel the most comfortable with, I am more than interested."

She thought he might have to consider his options for a while, but before she finished speaking he was already reaching for the button on his jeans.

"Take off your top," he ordered.

So. It wasn't that he was saving himself forever. Or that he had taken a permanent vow of chastity, which would've been a dreadful waste—at least in her opinion.

But...

Janey glanced out the kitchen window, the one with no curtains and a wide-open view into the backyard. "You mind if we take this somewhere else?"

"Right here," Len demanded. "Face me. No one can see anything anyway. Not unless they're sitting in the top branches of your apple tree."

He was lowering his zipper, the sound of the metal rasping loudly in the suddenly quiet room. She undid the work belt around her hips, laying it on the counter before turning back. She caught him in the process of shedding his T-shirt, reaching over his head to jerk the fabric forward and off his arms, revealing his massive chest. His biceps were like bricks, and his abdomen so structured she couldn't wait to run her fingers over the muscles to prove they were real. "How did you get such a gorgeous body?"

His grin widened, but he snapped his finger at her. "I don't see a hell of a lot of stripping going on."

"You want to help me?" she asked.

He shook his head. "You do this my way. I want your shirt off. Now."

A delicious shiver went up her spine as she tugged her T-shirt out of her work pants. His eyes locked on her fingers, and she took the time to inch the fabric upward. Moving slowly to reveal her bra before taking the shirt off over her head.

His breathing had increased in tempo as he stared in admiration at her chest. "Nice."

Janey licked her lips. "What now?"

Staring at him was a delicious experience. His broad chest and arms and shoulders were full of flexing muscles as he eased his jeans open, lowering them far enough the lovely band muscles that wrapped from his groin around his hips grew more visible.

A little sound of need escaped her. She wanted to touch *so* badly.

"Take off your pants," he demanded.

This time she didn't bother to tease. She dropped her pants and her drawers all in one motion, so eager to obey she forgot she still had work boots on. Everything became trapped at her ankles.

Len didn't seem to care. He closed the short distance between them and picked her up, placing her on the countertop next to her work belt. His strong hands rested on the naked swells of her butt.

He rested their foreheads together, both of them breathing shakily as they stared into each other's eyes. "You're killing me," Len confessed.

"Don't stop now." Janey was ready for anything except him stopping.

Only he did stop. Sort of. Stepped away and left her with nothing but the faint memory of his hands on her body and an aching need inside.

"Open your knees and let me see your pussy." Len's voice broke as she rushed to obey him. Rewarded by his groan of pleasure, she looked into his eyes as he dragged his gaze up her body.

"Let me see you too," she begged.

He had reached into his briefs, hand curling around his cock to stroke it. His hands were hidden from her sight under the fabric, but she knew exactly what he was doing. She slipped her own hands downward without any orders on his part. No way could she stop because joining in was too damn hot to miss.

She'd done this often enough to be a pro. The masturbating, not the doing it in front of another person—that part was brand new. Opening herself to his view as she dipped her fingers into the moisture he'd gotten started with just a kiss. Fingertips wet, she moved back to her clit and circled slowly with enough pressure to tease as she waited eagerly for him to do the next thing.

"God." Len squeezed his eyes shut, his hand motion stilling as he grimaced.

She couldn't decide if she should jump off the counter and rip down his pants so she could actually see what was happening like she wanted, or if she should just enjoy the show like it was, because while he might not believe it, she'd never seen anything so sexy in her life.

Him fighting so hard for control, striving to hold back his body's response made her that much hotter, that much quicker.

"Feels so good. *Oh*, Len. It feels so good. I can't wait until it's you actually touching me. Or licking me."

A feral growl escaped him. Len stopped what he was doing for long enough to shove his pants off his hips, his cock leaping free of his briefs. The long, thick length rebounded towards his rock-hard abdomen, his jeans hanging at mid-thigh. Janey whimpered and increased her tempo as he leaned against the counter opposite her and wrapped his fingers around the heavy shaft. His eyes were fixed on her fingers as she rubbed them over her clit.

He stroked, slowly but with a firm grip. She watched him rock his hips forward, fucking his hand with growing speed as she gasped in pleasure. Increasing the pressure she applied as she imagined every time he rocked forward, his cock brushed her clit.

No dirty words filled her ears—not from her soft-spoken Len. No commands to get herself off with her fingers, or suggestions about how he was going to shove his cock into her and fuck her until she couldn't walk. But what they were doing was so seriously filthy without any words, she was glad for the silence. The quiet broken only by heavy breathing, little moans of pleasure from her, and deep groans escaping his lips. Add in the wet sounds of her fingers and the slap of skin on skin from his fist—oh, yeah, it was hotter than hell.

Four feet separated them, but the setting was as intimate as if they'd been touching. His eyes never left her pussy except to feast on the rest of her body. She wasn't even completely naked, and he was looking at her as if he'd never seen anything so beautiful.

And she didn't know what to look at as he handled himself. His chest? His abs? His cock? The way his thighs tightened on every forward motion? Or the way his breathing made his entire body move, desperate need in every rock.

"*Oh!*"

Her climax hit, the tingling sensation that had been building changed so rapidly from nearly there to overwhelming, she gasped. Her gaze remained fixed on Len as his body shuddered, and he came. A strong stream shot upward against his belly as he pumped again and again until shuddering forward, curling around himself. He sucked in a deep breath, cursing lightly as he exhaled.

Janey was covered with sweat, Len's upper body as well. They both had their pants partway on, partway off, and she still wore her bra.

Amusement rolled through her along with satisfaction. "Well now, that was a first."

He turned his head toward her, his body still bent over as he braced himself with a hand on one knee. His grin twisted wryly. "Smartass."

Laughter bubbled up. "I didn't mean that way, but...yeah. I guess."

He grabbed his T-shirt and used it to wipe off his belly, hauling his jeans over his hips before moving toward her. She was still splayed bonelessly over the counter by the time he reached her.

Len caught her by the chin and kissed her tenderly. She resisted the temptation to tease or to get him heated up. It was time to savour the moment of closeness. A different kind of intimacy now than before.

It certainly wasn't what she had expected that afternoon, and it wasn't where she wanted them to end up, but the journey was sure turning out to be a whole hell of a lot of fun.

Chapter Six

SUDDENLY IT seemed as if the entire world was conspiring against them. Len had barely had time to talk to Janey on the telephone, let alone get a chance to be alone with her.

Some of it was her fault. She'd realized she needed some supplies, and made a trip to Calgary. She stayed the night with her parents, then brought home an enormous load of material in the back of the truck.

In spite of his best intentions to help her unload, Len found himself crazy busy as he got called out on one tow-truck request after another.

They all took turns driving pickups for the garage, and his name had come up on the roster. He didn't feel right trying to trade off with any of his brothers because that would've required telling them what he intended, or at least putting up with their teasing when they made assumptions about why he was trying to free his schedule.

The only good part was none of the towing involved serious accidents. It was always rough to have to help friends out of the ditch, knowing the unexpected expenses for vehicle repair were probably going to set them back. But when it was an actual accident, Thompson and Sons got called too, with ambulance and police on the scene...

Those were Len's least favourite moments to deal with.

Still, splitting his time between the shop and the tow truck kept him busy enough days passed without them getting together. Plus, he didn't want to push Janey. He figured she'd call when she was done with her latest rush of work. Only the longer she didn't make contact, the more he worried something was up.

Enough was enough. He was done his turn behind the wheel as of that evening. Troy got to put in the hours next.

It was his brother Mitch's fiancée who lit a fire under him, intentionally or not, he wasn't sure.

The set of red and blue lights flashing behind him as he dragged another vehicle back to the shop set his heart thumping as he wondered for a second what he was getting pulled over for.

Luckily Anna Coleman wasn't the type to tease too hard. She parked the RCMP car behind him and made her way up to his window, removing her sunglasses and offering a big smile. "Don't worry, no ticket. I wanted to get in touch with you in person."

"You need to get a new coloured light to turn on. Something to warn us it's a social call," Len suggested.

She laughed. "Mitch would like that too. The trouble for him is now every time he sees an RCMP behind his motorcycle, he thinks it's me. The guys down at the station are ragging on him because he accidentally blew a kiss at Magnus one time."

Len hooted. "Mitch didn't tell us about that."

"Oh really? Oops." She winked before her expression turned more serious. "Did something go wrong between you and Janey?"

He shook his head, not sure what she was talking about. "Not that I know of."

Anna hesitated. "Okay. So this is me telling tales on your girlfriend, then. I was doing neighbourhood patrol last night, and I swear I saw her sleeping in the back of her truck."

"What?" Len couldn't believe his ears. "Why would she do that? Was she on the street, or in her backyard?"

"Parked in her back driveway, so it's not as dangerous as if she were at the side of the road somewhere, but it didn't make sense to me. And while I know her, and could ask her if there were problems, I thought I'd check with you first. If she needs a place to stay—"

"I'll look into it," Len promised. Why the heck was Janey sleeping in her truck? "Thanks for telling me."

"Let me know if I can do anything to help." Anna checked the road behind her, then offered Len a final wave. "Mitch and I will see you at the barbecue tonight, right?"

"We'll be there."

He drove back to the shop, his brain full of more questions than he knew what to do with. He checked in with Clay, but they were nearly done their tasks for the morning. Which meant he had time to skip lunch and head straight to Janey's to find out what the hell was going on.

Her backyard was full of lumber, and she was in full-speed motion, installing vertical posts for a deck.

As soon as she spotted him, though, she put aside her tools and straightened, one hand going to her back as she stretched. "Hey. They haven't worked you to the bone yet."

Len marched right up and loomed over her, checking her carefully. She had dark marks under her eyes, and even as he examined her, she broke out into a full-fledged yawn. "You're working too hard," he snapped.

Her face folded into a frown. "Job won't get done if I don't do it."

This was the stubborn Janey who drove him crazy in the bad way. "Working around the clock won't get the job done any faster. You'll get hurt."

"I know what I'm doing."

He glared. Wondered for a moment how hard to push, then decided to hell with. He was mad, and she might as well know it. "You don't like sleeping in your house anymore?"

She paused, and then managed to look guilty and adorable at the same time. "Goddamn small-town gossip. Who told you?"

"Doesn't matter. Why'd you sleep in your truck?"

Janey flipped a hand toward the house. "I did the floors, and they stink to high heaven. They'll be good in another three days, but right now it's too toxic to go inside. That's why I'm working on the deck."

"And that's why you're sleeping in the back of your damn truck? Why didn't you ask to crash somewhere else?"

Janey planted her fists on her hips. "Right. So who am I going to crash with, Len? Katy's got a house full, Liz isn't back from holidays, and Shannon has a cat."

"Bullshit on Katy having no room. She's your best friend, and you know she'd always find a way to make room. Especially to stop you from doing something unsafe like sleeping in your truck."

She lost some of her bluster. "Well, maybe I didn't want to bother her."

"Fine, but stupid. What about my place?"

"That doesn't work because—" The most adorable flush spread over her cheeks, and she pinned her lips together as if refusing to say anything else.

It would have been more amusing if his blood wasn't still pounding hard enough to make his ears hum. "Because you don't want to sleep in my apartment? You'd prefer to camp out on a mattress in the back of your truck, where you've got no way to lock up and stay safe, rather than spend the night with me?"

"Oh, good grief," Janey complained. "It's not like that."

He reined in his anger with an iron will. "Good to know. Then I'll see you when you're done work for the day. Or did you want me to come here and help you finish up once I'm done?"

She stood silently for a moment, as if trying to figure out what he had just told her. "Why would you come here?"

"So I can help you put the tools away, and you can come home with me."

She wasn't fighting him anymore. Now it was more as if she was playing out mentally the directions the evening might turn. And he totally understood, because he was going there himself.

"I didn't want to inconvenience you," Janey started.

Enough. Len covered her mouth with his so she had to stop talking. He kissed her because it was either that or give her a good solid shouting at, and he didn't shout. Not often.

Even as she softened under him, it took a hell of a lot to lose his anger. He had his fingers fisted in her ponytail, the long length wrapped around his hand as he held her in place so he could ravish her lips. She moved in tight, as if seeking forgiveness with her touch as she slid her hands along his biceps and up to his shoulders. Scratching her nails lightly down his back.

He broke off the kiss, determined to make his point. "Just because I gave you an option doesn't mean I'm not planning on making it happen. Or that I'm not planning on taking care of you, like you should've let me in the first place. You want to meet at my house, or do you want me to come here?"

She was damn near vibrating. The words she was holding back—he wasn't sure if they were more in the line of "fuck you" or "I'm sorry, it will never happen again".

But she took a deep breath and settled herself a little before answering. "I'll come to your place. I don't know what time I'll be done, but it might be earlier than you."

He dug in his pocket and pulled out his keys, finding the one for his apartment and taking it off the chain. He handed it over. "If I'm not there, let yourself in."

"I can make something for the potluck tonight—"

"Dammit, Janey. Let yourself in, take a shower and hit the sack if that's what you need. I've got no agenda that I'm following, so stop trying to do the right thing, or whatever the hell it is you're doing."

That's when he fully expected to see her blaze up, but the sheer tiredness on her face told a different story. She nodded and accepted the key, tucking it in her pocket. "You're a bossy bastard."

The familiar complaint brought a smile to his face for the first time during the entire conversation. "So you've said before."

"It bears repeating occasionally."

He stroked her cheek softly. She might not like the idea, but if they were going to do this thing, they were going to do it right. And that meant she had to understand he was going to help take care of her.

Whether that made him a bossy bastard or not.

SHE CAUGHT herself yawning for the third time in a row and gave up.

For a short while after Len stopped over, she'd had plenty of energy. A combination of adrenaline, sexual frustration and guilt.

She'd known he wouldn't like her camping out in her truck, but after all the years she'd spent chasing him, the new revelation the other day had changed things.

Oh, she still wanted to jump his bones in a bad way, but she didn't want to be as assertive as she'd been. Assuming she could crash at his place seemed far too forward, and the last thing she wanted anymore was to make him feel pressured.

Janey carried her tools to the storage shed, stacking them neatly on the shelves before going back to do the final cleanup on her workspace. Scrap lumber got thrown into the back of her truck to take to the barbecue at Katy and Gage's that night.

Just looking at the hard metal made her body ache. Good thing she didn't have to sleep in there again tonight.

She packed clothes, rapidly stuffing things into a bag as she attempted not to breathe too many of the fumes inside the house. A couple minutes' work made sure all the upstairs windows were open to let the place air before she headed for her truck, and Len's place.

Letting herself in felt strange. Janey dropped her bag on the sofa, looking around with new eyes since the last time she'd been there. It was hard to believe it had been less than two weeks. So much had happened in that time, including...

The look of disappointment and frustration she'd spotted in Len's eyes popped to mind, and a sense of guilt rushed in, because he'd been right. She'd made some assumptions, and fixing things before they got to be problems was important.

She grabbed her phone and put a call through to her best friend. "I'm at Len's," she announced.

"Umm..." Katy sounded very confused.

God, Janey was so tired she wasn't thinking straight anymore. "Sorry. I didn't call to freak you out. Didn't want you to be worried if you go by the house and see the lights are all off."

Katy was smiling. Janey could tell, even over the phone. "Of course you didn't call me to freak me out, but don't try to lie and tell me it's not a nice bonus result."

"I solemnly swear not to tell you any details that will hit your ick factor." Janey stripped off her clothes and headed for the shower. "And I need to apologize. I made a mistake yesterday. Len pointed it out and gave me shit.

And while it's nothing you need to worry about, it made me think about how glad I am you're my friend."

"Awwww. That's so sweet." There were voices in the background behind Katy. "And I don't know what brought that on, but you're an awesome friend too, and I love you to pieces. And if you ever need anything, you let me know."

Janey made a smooching noise towards the phone.

Katy echoed her back. "I've got to run—getting things ready for the barbecue. Talk to you tonight?"

"Deal."

She hung up, laying her phone on the bathroom counter and turning on the water in the shower. She stepped under the spray and turned her face upward, and let the exhaustion roll off her with the water droplets.

She *had* made a mistake. Damage control might be done with Katy, but she still had to fix it with Len. But not until she worked out that kink from sleeping on a thin camping mattress in the back of the truck. And not until she'd snuck in a nap of at least thirty minutes. That should be enough to refresh her before Len came home.

By the time she got out and dried off, she barely had enough energy left to grab Len's shirt off the hook on the bathroom door, tug it over her head and crawl under the quilt.

Chapter Seven

THE LIGHT had changed.

Janey rolled over and cracked her eyes opened, groggily searching her memory for where she was.

Len's place—thankfully with all memories intact this time, even the ones that made her flush with embarrassment. Her gaze darted to the window to check to see if the sky was still bright.

Instead, she got caught in a pair of dark brown eyes, smooth warm chocolate brown that made her hungry.

Len lay beside her, his head propped up on his hand, his elbow resting on the mattress. She glanced down to discover he was lying on top of the covers fully dressed.

"You just get home?"

His lips twisted slightly. "Is it too creepy to say I've been here for at least ten minutes?"

She laughed. "It's your bed, you're allowed to be in it."

"Damn right I am."

He rolled over and kissed her. The whole long length of him pressing her to the mattress, and even with the quilt and his clothes between them, Janey felt a pulse of sexual tension leap into her belly.

This wasn't like the afternoon when he'd basically chastised her with his kiss. This was exploration, and tender, his lips moving over hers softer than the water from the showerhead had rushed over her skin. Janey wiggled her arms free so she could reach up and thread her fingers through his hair.

Len kissed the tip of her nose before pulling away. "I like finding you in my bed," he admitted.

Sadly, he rolled off. She was ready to protest until he caught the top of the quilt and peeled it down, exposing her from head to toe.

"Damn. I should have hid all my T-shirts," he complained. She smiled but she was far too breathless to laugh. He rested his fingers over her lips. "You and me, we need to finish that talk we started this afternoon."

His hand slid down to trace back and forth along her collarbones.

"I'm sorry I didn't ask for your help," Janey said.

He nodded once. "Accepted. But let's make this clear. Just because I don't have experience in one area doesn't mean I don't have a hell of a lot of opinions and needs and abilities. I'm not a two-year-old, and you treating me like I am is going to backfire big time."

"Of course you're a man, but I'm not helpless," she countered, "You're right, though, I did make some assumptions. I won't do that to you again. But, Len? While we're getting stuff out in the open?"

He rested his hand on her upper arm, sliding his palm up and down against her naked skin. "Yeah?"

"You're not a big talker. And I don't expect you to change, but you gotta know there's a difference between staying silent because there's nothing you want to add to the conversation, and staying silent because you're refusing to share."

He nodded.

And then with typical Len restraint, he caught hold of the bottom of the T-shirt she wore and tugged it until she had to curl up and let him strip her bare.

Her heart fluttered, anticipation tingling through her like a fine mist of rain.

This was all up to him. Janey liked sex, and she liked being an active participant, but she was going to do her damnedest to take her cues from him and see which way he wanted to go. No more pushing, but no more assuming.

He pressed her back to the mattress, his hand slipping off her shoulder and down her torso, his fingers along the outside of her breast as his thumb came to a stop over her nipple. The sensitive tip reacted like he'd hit the remote control button, pebbling tight.

Len seemed fascinated with her body's response. "You still sleepy?" he asked.

"Hell, no." The words came out breathless, turning into a deep gasp as he leaned over and licked the nipple nearest him.

Janey let her head relax back into the pillow. Chances were he would take his time exploring, and she had absolutely no issues with that.

With her eyes closed, it was easy to concentrate on the sensations. Focus on what it felt like when he closed his lips and sucked. One hand continued to caress her breast, playing with her nipple before releasing it in a slow sensual tease.

Every draw of his lips increased the web of sensation tangling around her body. He changed position, and she waited for him to come back to her lips, but he changed sides, continuing to torment her other breast until she found herself grabbing his hair and damn near purring as she tried to…

She didn't know what she wanted. Shove him away or keep him right where he was.

Fortunately, Len seemed to know what he wanted. He met her gaze square on, his chocolate eyes melting with passion. "You okay with me touching you everywhere?"

"Is *oh, hell yeah* clear enough?"

He chuckled, the noise coming from farther down the bed as the mattress shifted. Kisses started again, this time beginning with one pressed to the tip of the nipple he had left throbbing. One landed on the underside of her breasts followed by a set across her belly until he reached her bellybutton. Not just his lips, but the side of his face with his five o'clock shadow scraping her skin, and she shivered.

Len tongued her belly, sending more thrills through her. "You know how many times I've wanted to do this?"

She was pretty sure he'd figured out that scratchy layer on his chin was driving her crazy, because even while he flicked his tongue in and out of her belly button, he teased her with his chin. His hands rested lightly on both hips to hold her down.

"Don't stop," Janey begged.

It seemed she'd been doing a lot of that around him, considering how short a time they'd officially been going out.

Luckily he wasn't finished. He slid a hand down to separate her curls, changing position, and she couldn't resist wiggling up on her elbows to watch.

His expression? Better than a kid being handed the biggest present under the Christmas tree. Len caressed his hand over her mound, fingers towards her belly button, the heel of his hand right over where she needed him, but not with enough pressure. Not yet.

Should she offer suggestions? He'd told her not to treat him like he was incapable, but she knew not every guy got it right the first time without some guidance. And every woman liked different things. Heck, she liked different things depending on what day it was—there was no use in being shy.

So she did what felt right and pulled her knees apart, exposing herself to anything he wanted to do.

Len cursed softly, grip tightening as he swallowed hard. "I'm trying to go slow, but damn if I can any longer."

He used both hands to open her fully to his gaze, settling in and caressing with his thumbs. Just for a moment before his head dropped and blocked her view.

Janey was back to nothing but sensations, but *oh, God,* the sensations were so damn good. He might be inexperienced, but he found her clit no problem, teasing it with the tip of his tongue perfectly before widening the circle of pleasure, then dipping deeper.

"Use your fingers on me too, if you want," Janey coached. "If you play with my clit, I'll come. But if your fingers are inside me while you play, or your cock, I'll come even harder."

"Gotcha."

His hand left her hip and he went back to eating her hungrily, but now there was an added bonus. A ghostly touch explored. Lightly, then more boldly as moisture from her body covered his fingers and eased his way.

He lifted up to watch her face as he pushed a finger into her. Stopping deep inside as if memorizing the sensation.

"More," she ordered.

He nodded, playing slowly, the pad of his fingertip brushing the front of her passage as he worked in and out. It was a strange sensation, more intense than she thought it should be.

Not that she was complaining, not at all.

He did it again, this time with two fingers. Two very thick fingers, with thick calluses, and maybe that made the difference because, *whoa Nelly*, the rubbing bit was doing things she hadn't expected.

"Good?" he asked.

Janey nodded, checking to see how he was doing. "Very good. You want to take off your clothes?"

He shook his head. "Later."

Oh, well then. That was fine too.

And like some practiced virtuoso on the piano, Len combined his new tricks. He kept up the fingering motion and resumed tormenting her with his mouth.

He might not be a big talker, but he was damn good with his tongue. The familiar precursor of pleasure rocketed closer at high-speed. That strange internal massage combined with the flick of his tongue in exactly the right place—inspiring. His lips closed around her clit, and he sucked, the entire bed swaying with the motion of his hand.

Janey planted her feet on the bed and rocked against him in time with his finger thrusts, a low moan of approval escaping her lips.

The moan changed to an outright cry of satisfaction as she came, hips coming up off the bed with the force of it as he worked her past the initial bloom. Janey stroked her fingers through his hair, tugging him away when she needed him to ease off.

He stilled his fingers, but the bed kept shaking for another bit, and she glanced down in time to Len's face clench as he came, hips pressed against the mattress.

He breathed out a satisfied sigh and laid his cheek on her hipbone. "And don't you dare think or say anything about *poor me*, because I'm damn happy right now."

Janey laughed. "Well, that makes two of us then."

He tilted his head. "We're not done," he warned.

"I hoped you'd say that," she answered back, her own smile reflecting the one on his face. "And I'm not saying *poor you*, but I do think your day will only get better as it goes along."

The anticipation in his eyes—

Good thing she'd had that nap. They were both going to need all the energy they could muster.

IT WAS a dilemma he'd never faced before. He desperately needed a shower because they had the damn barbecue in an hour's time. But all he wanted was to turn around and end up back in bed.

He'd lasted longer than he'd expected with the taste of her flooding his system. The touch of her soft skin under his palms.

Dirt talk from the guys during drinks occasionally included complaining about having to go down on their girls to get them to reciprocate. Len had heard his brothers call the others out for being stupid jackasses. He'd always stayed quiet—like usual, so no one had said anything—but now he could agree one hundred percent.

Every one of those complainers had to be absolute idiots. Maybe he didn't need to eat. Maybe he could survive on sex alone. He'd be willing to try.

Janey didn't suffer from the same inability to make a decision he did. She crawled off the mattress, a wide grin firmly planted on her face, which made him feel all the more cocky since he was the one who'd put it there.

"I'll see you in the shower," she said.

He stripped down, tossing his things in the laundry basket. In the distance, the water turned on and instantly images of Janey with water-slicked skin leapt to mind.

It wasn't his imagination. Nope. He'd seen the real thing before, been dreaming about it at night, and now she stood only ten paces away. All he had to do was walk forward and join her.

His cheeks were going to be sore from grinning.

He might have just come, but his cock was hardening again, and when he stepped through the bathroom door to discover she'd left the shower curtain partway open, hands moving slowly over her body as she smiled at him—

"I like a man with a good recovery time," Janey teased.

He stepped into the tub, eager to explore this time instead of having to hold back. "It's not the recovery time I'm worried about."

She laughed, wrapping her arms around him. The fronts of their bodies came in contact, his cock a solid rock between them, pressing against her soft belly. Janey lifted her lips, and he dove into the kiss. Soaking in the taste of her as he let his hands explore.

Soft skin, warm and wet. Tantalizing. Addictive.

She ran her hands over his ass and his hips moved instinctively, rubbing against her.

"I have a suggestion," she offered, her hands continuing to torment him as she dragged her fingernails lightly over his ass cheeks.

"I'm all ears."

"You're all cock," she teased as she snuck her hand between them. He sucked for air as she caught him in her fist. "There are so many things I want to do to you."

No way her list could be longer than the one he'd been mentally making for years. "No rush. And no objections either."

Janey moved her hand back, pulling his foreskin up then pressing down slowly. Not enough pressure to make him go off, which was good because he was on a hair trigger. "Let's do it."

"Do it—what? Have sex? Now?"

She stroked him as she nodded. "I'm wet and ready, you're definitely ready, and I can't wait to have you inside me."

Jeez. At this rate he was going to last three seconds.

He opened his mouth to protest, but she'd popped out of the shower and grabbed a towel. "Come on, you're cleaned up and it's not going to get any easier the longer we wait."

She darted back into the bedroom, her butt cheeks flexing as she crawled onto the bed, glancing over her shoulder and wiggling her brows.

The small part of his brain that was still functioning registered he had to grab a condom. He snagged up the box he'd bought only that week, and grabbed one out.

He might be inexperienced, but he was still going to make this good for her. He crowded her to the mattress, letting her pull him down so they were naked, skin to skin, the water droplets clinging to them squeezed to a thin slick of moisture.

She broke away from the kiss he'd begun, eying him for a moment before speaking softly. "I'm not suggesting I be in charge all the time, but I read something, and if you're interested…"

She pulled the condom from his fingers.

"If you intend on putting that on me, we're gonna be done before we get started," he warned.

Janey pulled her knees apart and his hips settled over hers, his cock resting against her mound. "Fuck me like this. Don't go inside me this time, but rub my clit. That way you don't need a condom, and we both get to feel really good."

"Janey—"

"I don't care if you come after three strokes, but I saw this and it looked damn hot, so stop complaining and do it."

It wasn't her suggestion he was going to protest, it was not doing anything else beforehand. But when she rocked against him, he rocked back, and it felt so fucking good there was no way he could stop.

He pushed up on his arms so the only place they connected was his cock thrusting over her pussy lips, moisture coating him on every move. She was hot, and wet, and oh-so-willing as she lifted her hips and helped.

"Oh, *yes*, that feels wonderful." Janey put her hands on her breasts and played with her nipples, and a shot of lust roared through him.

There was too much to see, too much to *feel* as the tingling sensation in his balls increased. He adjusted position, kneeling slightly so he could rock against her at a sharper angle. Watching with fascination as his cock slid over her clit again and again.

It was so different than his hand. Different, but amazing and unbelievable, and more than he could take for very long.

She whimpered slightly as he pressed harder, the head of his cock sliding over her belly on every thrust. "You close?" she asked.

Len couldn't answer because he was holding his breath to try to last—and then he couldn't answer because he was groaning out his release, stopping with his hips thrust forward so his seed landed on her belly. He might have come less than fifteen minutes earlier, but somehow he had more than enough left to leave splattered lines shooting to her belly button and over her flat stomach toward her breasts.

Len looked up to discover she was grinning wildly.

"You didn't come," he scolded.

"I came before, and that was hot." She grabbed a tissue from beside his bed to wipe her belly. Then she grabbed hold of his biceps and tugged him up the bed to a seated position. "And we're not done."

He was going to die from pleasure. "More?"

"More," she insisted.

He might have a good recovery time, but he'd already come twice. "Optimist."

"I have faith in you." And damn if she didn't wrap her hands around his cock. Gently, thank God, because Len wasn't sure how much more his dick could take at this point.

But she stroked him softly as she pressed her body to his, lips connecting. Too many sensations, Len had thought before, and they just weren't stopping.

Her breasts rubbed against his body as her hand continued to move. Their tongues tangled, breaths mingling. Len was reduced to nothing but heat and the blood pounding through his veins as she brought a response far too quickly.

Enough waiting. He wanted her. Len lowered his hands to cup her ass, lifting her into his lap, her knees on either side of his body. "I want inside you, now."

Janey caught up the condom from where she'd abandoned it on the bed, ripping the package open and rolling the latex down his shaft.

It had to be said. "You're a genius, by the way."

She rose onto her knees, glancing up briefly with laughter in her eyes. "I wanted you to enjoy this."

"It's possible to not enjoy sex?"

His heart was pounding as if he'd been working like a dog lifting engine blocks out of a vehicle without a hoist. She angled his cock back, and heat wrapped around the tip. Slowly she undulated her hips, taking him into her body as he fought the urge to simply drive upward.

He was a man of few words, but there were some classic phrases scrolling through his brain right then. *Holy fuck* was the most coherent. By the time she was fully seated in his lap, and he was fully seated in her, Len was feeling lightheaded.

Janey caught him around the neck, forehead resting against his as she stared into his eyes. "Good?"

He nodded, unable to speak.

"You want me to do the moving? Or whenever you're ready to roll, go for it. It feels amazing to have you inside me," she confessed.

Did he want her to do the moving? His hands cupped her ass and he lifted her slightly, flexing his biceps with little effort to raise her up so the head of his cock clung to her passage. He brought her down slowly, savouring the sensation of heat and pressure. Again, so different from his hand, or hers. So perfect that he repeated the move. Increasing the tempo as she hugged his shoulders, her teeth biting into her lower lip as he fucked her. The tingling pleasure of another orgasm was rising, but not nearly as quickly as he'd worried about.

He paused to take her lips, dropping one hand to caress her breasts as he pulsed lightly within her, relishing the connection between them. He had wanted this forever, so for however long he got to enjoy it, he would appreciate every moment.

Janey wiggled, rubbing against his pubic bone. He broke away from her lips, still controlling their positioning to move her back far enough to reach between them.

The instant his thumb hit her clit she gasped. "Oh. *Oh my...*"

He didn't have to ask her if it was good—the way she squeezed tight around him was a clear indication. The pressure also made him damn near see stars.

Control firmly in place for a little longer, he sped up his fingers over her clit, and soaked in every gasp, every moan that escaped her until she clawed his shoulders, hard, her pussy a tight fist around his cock.

"Oh, hell, *yes.*" Her head dropped against his chest as she shook, pulsing pressure seizing him like she'd never let go.

He couldn't hold back any longer. Len twisted her and took her to the mattress under him to thrust easier. Driving in as her passage held him in a vise. Bringing the pressure up until along with her moans of pleasure, he was panting, every rock forward making them both gasp until he exploded.

Pleasure shot through his body as the heat continued and she writhed under him. Len's brain went temporarily off-line. There was too much going on. Too much pleasure to focus on only one aspect of it. From his balls, to his dick, to the quivering in his muscles, happy endorphins danced all the way to his brain.

Janey linked her hands behind his neck and all but jerked him on top of her, their sweaty bodies making contact as she kissed him wildly.

He rolled to the side to avoid crushing her, and she rolled with him until she ended up on top. His cock still deep inside her pussy. Bodies shaking as they tried to catch their breaths.

Len didn't know how long they lay there as he stroked her hair and let the pleasure continue to rock him for as long as he could.

Finally, Janey pressed her palms to his chest and eased up enough her brilliant smile lit his world. "If I say thank you for sharing that experience with me, is that too weird?"

He shook his head. For his first time, the sex had been good. *Damn good*—made so much better since it was with Janey. But still... "Timing was off."

A bright laugh broke free from her lips, her honey brown eyes sparkling. "That whole simultaneous-orgasm thing? Number one, I don't think it happens as often as the books or movies say. And number two, it's all about enjoying ourselves. Trust me, I enjoyed that a hell of a lot."

Which was good, because Len had enjoyed it a hell of a lot as well.

Chapter Eight

TWENTY MINUTES later they were both still grinning.

She rested her head on Len's shoulder briefly, her body swaying as they bumped down the gravel driveway to Katy's house. He curled his arm around her, stroking her arm with his fingers exactly right to send shivers rolling along her spine.

It was as if now that the dam had burst, Len was intent on making up for lost time. What he lacked in experience, he more than made up for in enthusiasm. Janey figured the sex was only going to get better and better, and it hadn't sucked in the first place.

Plus, he still had a few other firsts she really wanted him to enjoy. She'd be keeping her eyes open for more opportunities to rock his world...

But tonight was a time for family and friends—the traditional Thompson family summer barbecue. Janey had been coming to the event for years as Katy's friend. Being there this time as Len's lover made it a whole new ballgame.

She tried to find something to discuss that wasn't about sex, or thoughts about going home to his bed when the evening was over. "I finished all the prep work on the deck today," she told him. "So tomorrow I start laying deck boards."

"I'm off work from the garage. I'll give you a hand, if you want," Len offered.

"I'd like that," she admitted. "If you got an extra drill lying around, bring it with you."

Len put the truck in park beside the other Thompson vehicles. He chuckled softly, but didn't say anything else.

Janey followed him out the driver's side door. "What was that about?"

He paused for long enough to whisper in her ear. "You want to screw?"

He grabbed a cooler from the back of the truck, cradling it with one arm to leave his fingers free to link with hers.

Meanwhile, she fought the giggles. "Stop it."

"I could have sworn you just asked me to drill you."

They were both smiling pretty hard when they rounded the corner to the backyard. The rest of the family was already there along with a dozen or more neighbours. Janey gave Len's fingers a squeeze then let go, taking her own offering for the potluck toward the house. A long picnic table waited there, the surface already covered with casserole dishes.

Katy turned from organizing cutlery. "Hey, you finally made it."

"Umm, we had to…" Janey sputtered to a stop, floundering for words. It was too late to stop the heat that rushed to her cheeks.

Her best friend gave her a wink. "You're supposed to think of an excuse ahead of time, but trust me, there is no hiding the satisfaction on your face. I know why you're late."

Which meant everyone in the yard had probably figured out they couldn't keep their hands off each other. What the hell. And yet, she didn't really care if it was common knowledge they'd had sex before coming to the barbecue. All she cared about was that look of extreme pleasure in Len's eyes as he'd stared at her—before, during and after.

That was what mattered.

Janey grinned as she looked around the yard to see who was there. "Good turnout."

Katy nodded, sliding the tray of deviled eggs Janey had brought onto the picnic table. "It's nice to have the good weather and be able to have people outside. We need to do some major work inside the house before we can start having parties in the winter."

Janey made a face. "I would have loved to do that job. Why couldn't you have decided to change things up last year?"

"You still planning on heading to Calgary once you sell your house?" Katy asked.

Sadly, Janey nodded. "There is a lot more work in housing in the Calgary area, so even though I'd prefer to stay here, I don't see how I can make a go of it."

Not with the competition. Brad Jons had been trying to get a hold of her all week about *something important.* Janey admitted she'd been blowing off returning his calls. The guy himself was nice enough, but it was likely something to do with his uncle, and she couldn't get over her suspicions something weird was up there.

Besides, she now had other things to focus on. She let her gaze linger on Len.

"You're drooling."

She snapped up the bird at Katy, who simply laughed. "Just saying. That's a pretty contented smile on your face."

"Not much different from the one on yours." Janey checked out her friend. "You know I should hate you. You had a baby a month ago, and you look like this?" Janey gestured at the trim jeans and T-shirt Katy wore, no sign of baby body remaining.

"Hey, it's not as if I don't have plenty of opportunity to burn off calories." Katy pointed toward where her partner Gage was standing with the guys, their baby tucked into a snuggly on his chest. "I get a workout at night dealing with Tanner."

"And a workout with Gage anytime he can get you," Janey teased.

Katy's eyes grew wide. "I have no idea what you're talking about. There is no such thing as sex after kids, don't you know?"

111

"Ha! I called bullshit, but if that's true, all the more reason why I'm never procreating."

Her best friend smiled. "Yeah, we're having to be a little bit creative these days, but I'm not at all unhappy."

Creative was good.

Janey kept her mouth shut. Len's secret wasn't hers to share with anyone, especially not with her BFF. But in the coming days, she could totally see them using their creativity in the sack to satisfy everything Len had ever dreamed of doing.

Which would be fine with her. He hadn't mentioned the specifics of why he'd still been a virgin, but whatever had caused the delay hadn't held him back an hour ago.

She and Katy joined the group of women seated in lawn chairs in a circle by the fire pit. There were so many familiar faces. Janey waved at Shannon and Liz as she settled into the empty chair next to Nicole Adams.

"I didn't know you were back in town. Great to see you again," Janey offered.

The dark-haired woman offered a smile. "I'm back for good. School's done, and I got a job at the local law firm."

"Awesome." Janey glanced around the yard, her gaze lighting on Nicole's twin brother, Mike, discussing something seriously with Len's brother Troy. "I bet the family is glad to have you around."

Nicole nodded. "My Lord, you would've thought I had opened every one of their veins and left them to bleed out the way they carried on when I told them I was going away to school."

"I can believe it, only I got that reaction when I told my family I *wasn't* going away."

Two of them shook their heads in sympathy for each other. "It's tough at times to follow your own path, but it's worth it in the end," Nicole said. "I didn't want to work for the family feed mill my whole life. Doesn't mean I don't like spending time with them."

Janey agreed completely. "Exactly. It just means you want to have your own life."

They exchanged high fives. Nicole paused before raising a brow. "Hey. I heard this rumor about you and a certain quiet fellow. Is it true?"

Oh no, Janey wasn't falling for that one. "All depends what you've heard."

Nicole smiled. "And that's all I needed to know. It's as good as a confession."

"Shut up," Janey drawled, but she was smiling as she accepted the drink Katy offered her.

"I wanted to make sure of my facts." Nicole glanced around the yard. "Damn, the dating pool is getting shallower by the minute. Why did I decide to come back to Rocky Mountain House?"

"There are plenty of guys in town still."

Nicole held up fingers as she called out names. "Katy nabbed Gage—good one there, by the way. Anna Coleman must've used her handcuffs on Mitch. Now I see Len grinning like a fool, and it's all because of Janey here."

"There does seem to be something in the water," Katy teased. "You'd better be careful, or you'll be the next to fall prey to the Thompson charm."

Now that was an intriguing thought. "You got the oldest and youngest to pick from. Who's it going to be? Clay or Troy?" Janey offered up her best friend's brothers like sacrifices.

Nicole seemed to seriously consider the question, her gaze trailing over the two men. "Troy is best friends with my brother. I've seen the two of them going gaga over girls for too long to take him seriously. But Clay? He's one fine man. I'd take him any way I could, anytime."

Katy made a rude noise. "Forget I ever brought up the topic. What is it with you and Janey wanting to tell me about how sexy my brothers are? Gross."

Nicole and Janey exchanged amused glances. Teasing Katy was too tempting to resist.

Janey purred for a moment. "If you really want to watch someone squirm, just mention cock size and—"

"Good grief, you do that one more time, and I swear I will get even with you, Janey Watson." Katy glared threateningly.

Janey laughed as she got to her feet, ready to head farther into the yard. "That's my revenge for all the disgusting things you shared about pregnancy and childbirth."

Katy stuck out her tongue, but she was smiling.

Everyone at the party was familiar to Janey. She waved often, offering greetings as she slowly worked her way across the yard.

114

One of the good parts of living in one place her entire life—in some ways, she was always home. There was always that sense of the familiar, even if it was simply coming around a corner to bump into people she'd seen last week, and the week before. And the same people she'd see down the road. The consistency was something rock solid.

It kind of made up for the parts of familiarity that weren't as much fun.

She'd planned to sneak up on Len, but it was no use. She turned from chatting with a couple who'd recently returned to the area, and discovered his gaze on her. A satisfied smile tugged the corners of his mouth.

The entire way to his side, his eyes never left hers.

She snagged her hands around his elbow and tucked in close to his side.

"You keep looking at me like that and we'll have to find a shed or something to fool around in," she whispered, shivering as he rumbled in approval.

"If that was a threat, you need to change tactics." His lips brushed her cheek as he spoke softly in return.

Then damn if Clay didn't go and interrupt a lovely little daydream she was working up that involved sneaking away with Len. "How is Margaret doing?" he asked, his dark eyes steadfastly fixed on her.

It took a second for Janey to figure out what he was asking. "Oh, you mean Margaret and Cam? Haven't you talked to them yet? I thought you went to school with her."

Clay shrugged. "Haven't made it across the yard. I noticed you were over there with them, and thought I'd ask."

That was weird. "She's starting at the school in the fall, and he's with the public works department."

Len's brother shifted from side to side, nodding slowly before straightening up. "I need to grab something."

He vanished before she could figure out exactly what was so strange about the whole situation. She turned to Len, but his expression was as confused as hers must've been. "You have any idea what that was about?"

Len shook his head. "Clay isn't always the easiest person to understand."

They joined in conversation with another group, people's curiosity at the new relationship between them tempered by long-lasting friendships. People were used to seeing the two of them at events.

Them, together?

That was something slightly different, but in this group Janey felt safe. The teasing was all good-natured, and the lingering glances were more about gloating than anything else.

They found lawn chairs next to Gage and Katy for supper, baby Tanner gurgling contentedly in his car seat as Gage rocked him with his foot.

"You're good at that," Janey teased.

"Multitasking." Gage grinned. "We've learned if he's rocking, he's not squawking."

They filled paper plates with the potluck offerings. Burgers and casseroles. Twelve kinds of salad, and an endless array of squares. In the background, country music played loud enough to satisfy the good old boys gathered around Len's dad by the barbecue.

The sense of contentment in Janey's heart grew.

Len rested his hand on the back of her chair, his fingers playing over her shoulders and neck even as he used his other hand to dig into the feast precariously balanced in his lap.

Janey raised a brow at the sheer volume of food on his plate. "Do you always eat this much?"

Gage laughed loudly for a moment. "Sorry, but I thought for sure you knew. Len's a legend. He's been the champion of every eating contest I've ever attended since I met him."

"I'm a growing boy," Len joked.

"You are the biggest of all the Thompson boys," Janey agreed.

Katy shot forward in her lawn chair, covering her mouth and giving Janey a dirty look as she fought to swallow the sip of soda she'd just taken.

"What?" Janey asked.

Her friend leaned closer, dropping her voice to a whisper. "I swear you are such a brat."

Janey was totally lost until she remembered the earlier teasing about cock size, and this time it was her turn to scramble for air. "Oh my God, you have such a dirty mind. I wasn't talking about *that* at all."

The conversation kind of went downhill from there.

Happiness washed over the entire evening as Janey enjoyed the company of friends and the man at her side who couldn't seem to keep his hands off her.

Dusk was beginning to fall, and a fire had been lit. Roasting sticks and marshmallows appeared out of nowhere.

Len caught her fingers in his. "I have something to show you."

They strolled past Troy and Mike who were laughing uproariously about something. Troy gave her a wink, but other than that didn't bother to tease, which was good because she had an idea where Len was taking her, and she didn't want to be interrupted.

The garden shed at the back of the property. She knew it all too well from hiding out in it over the years with Katy when they were supposed to be doing chores.

Hmm. Would it be as good of a hideout to fool around in?

Len hauled the door open, glancing over her shoulder back into the yard. Janey peeked as well, pleased to see their escape had gone unwitnessed.

She was drawn into the darkness, and the door closed firmly behind her with a resolute *click*. She caught hold of Len's shoulders and eased against him. Strong hands wrapped around the back of her neck as he guided them together. Their lips made contact—a scalding-hot kiss that set her wiggling on the spot, craving more.

"You were driving me nuts," Len confessed. "Every time you rubbed against me, I got harder. I swear my cock is ready to explode."

118

Well, now. "We can't have random cock explosions interrupting the barbecue, can we?"

He jerked her shirt free from her pants, his big palms pressed to her skin. Sliding up, he shoved away her bra. Janey hummed in approval as he took hold of her breasts, his grip just on the right side of demanding. His fingers on her nipples, pinching them to sharp peaks.

The scent of earth and grass surrounded them as he shoved up her shirt and bent over to suck a nipple into his mouth. Hard and fast, an exquisite sensation to add to everything she'd enjoyed already that evening.

Janey threaded her fingers into his hair. "That feels so good."

He didn't answer, not with words. Simply switched sides and sucked. His hands continuing to caress and massage.

As much fun as his attention was, Janey had another idea burning up her brain. She caught hold of his belt and slipped the leather loose, the buckle rattling in the darkness. One more move released the button on his jeans before she caught hold of his zipper.

Len groaned. "Janey, I won't last."

"You need to get over that obsession." She carefully pulled the zipper over the heavy bulge in his briefs. Opening his jeans and sliding them partway off his hips as she settled on her knees. "You have a zero-to-sixty-in-under-three-seconds recovery rate, so who gives a damn how long you last?"

Janey gazed upward. Just enough light flowed in the small shed window for her to be able to see his eyes flash as he stared downward. She rubbed her cheek over his cock, the heat of his shaft passing through his briefs.

He swallowed hard.

She put her teeth against him, dragging down slowly until she had his balls under her lips. "I want to suck your cock. Can I, please?"

If she'd bet he would be shy to respond to her filthy request, she would have lost. He immediately caught the edge of his briefs and jerked the elastic down to release his cock.

He caught hold of his shaft by the base, his other hand slipping into her hair. "Lick your lips."

She hurried to obey, rolling her tongue over the surface and getting them wet. Before she could haul her tongue back, he surprised her, pressing the tip of his cock to her mouth and getting sideswiped.

A moan reverberated off the walls of the shed, so Janey did it again, swirling her tongue over him and taking in his taste. The hint of salt as precome gathered in the slit.

He used the grip he had on her hair to tug her away slightly. "Close your mouth."

Janey had both hands on his hips now, holding on tight as he played the head of his cock over her mouth, painting her lips with the moisture leaking from the tip. Then he pushed forward, opening her with his heavy shaft as he filled her mouth.

Oh, yes. She tightened around him as he retreated, adding suction to every move.

Len took control, rocking forward and back, fucking her mouth with infinite care. He pulled the hair back from her face, his fingers tender against her cheek as he angled her head more and continued to thrust forward.

Every chance she got she used her tongue. Her lips. Panting noises joined the heavy gasps escaping his lips.

"So fucking amazing," Len whispered.

His butt muscles clenched under her fingers, and she figured he was close. She increased the pressure on the next withdrawal, and he swore.

"*Janey...*"

When the first taste of his release splashed on her tongue, she leaned in as hard as possible, swallowing around him. That only dragged another curse free, this one a mash of syllables that made no sense in any language, but the meaning was completely clear. His thick length filled her mouth, her nose pressed to his rock-solid abdomen as he shook. His hips continuing to pulse forward.

Janey swallowed again and again, her body's aching need ignored because what she was doing was damn pleasurable all on its own.

He slammed a palm against the wall behind her, hovering over her as he gasped for air. Janey pulled back slowly, letting his cock go with a *pop*, coming back to lick his still semi-erect length. Leaving him with a kiss to the tip.

She rested on her heels, smiling upward. She must've looked like a cat that'd gotten into the cream. "You were awesome. And I won't even ask how you knew to hold my hair and stuff, because, hey, I have Internet too."

Satisfaction was damn near rolling off him. "That was a million times better than anything I've ever watched, because it was you."

"Awww. You're sweet." She winked. "And dirty, which I like. That was *so* much fun."

Len grinned. "That's my line."

He tugged her to vertical, catching her under her chin and kissing her passionately. She couldn't stop smiling, her lips curving against his until he had to stop kissing her and instead rested their foreheads together.

His dark chocolate gaze drifted over her face carefully. "Thank you."

"My pleasure."

"It will be," he promised. "As soon as we get home. I have so many things I want to do to you."

Janey helped him get dressed, because the sooner they rejoined the party, the sooner they could say goodbye. He was right. There were still so many firsts for them to enjoy.

Chapter Nine

THE WORK down at the shop hadn't changed, but the rest of Len's days were totally different.

"Hey, loverboy. Can you concentrate enough to finish this tune-up? Or do I need to send you home early in the hopes you eventually get this out of your system?"

Dammit. Len jerked himself back to attention. "Sorry."

Clay shook his head. "I get it, you're having a good time with Janey and all that, but try to keep your head together while you're here."

He held in his protests because his brother was right. He was distracted, and down at the shop wasn't the place to let his attention wander. So while he focused on the task in front of him, he attempted to put aside all the other things that had begun to fill his time.

Like Janey. Hanging out with her, and doing everything from dirt biking to canoeing. And yes, having sex, including everything he'd ever dreamed of, and a few things she'd suggested that blew his mind.

It wasn't as if they were fooling around *all* the time. He was working, and she was working extra long hours to make her deadline of putting the house up for sale before the summer was out.

But she wasn't sleeping at the construction site much anymore.

She hadn't moved in with him, but when they finished exhausting themselves in bed, she tended to roll over, and Len would put an arm around her and cuddle her in tight.

If they woke up together in the morning more often than not, he couldn't find much in him to regret it. This wasn't going to last forever, but while it did, he'd make sure they both enjoyed it as much as possible.

Only he definitely was distracted. Enough that guilt set in, and when Clay asked for someone to help with a last-minute late-night job, Len put up his hand.

Mitch's jaw dropped. "You?"

"Shut up."

Clay cracked a grin as he wiped the oil off his hands with a rag. "I'd argue you out of it, but you're old enough to know your own mind. If you need any help give me a shout, but otherwise I'm out of here."

"Me too," Troy offered. "Mike and I are headed up to Red Deer, if anybody wants to join us."

"Don't drive home if you've been drinking," Clay warned, his face folding into a frown as he stared at his younger brother.

Troy shot him a dirty look. "Gee, Mom, I've never heard that before. What do you think, Clay? That I'm stupid?"

"I think when you get together with Mike, you don't think," Clay snapped.

"Get over it." Troy shoved in the drawer on the wrench cabinet harder than necessary, the tools rattling with a loud clang. "I won't do anything reckless, but maybe you should for a change."

Clay folded his arms over his chest. "What the hell does that mean?" he demanded.

Troy shook his head as he headed toward the door. "Forget it, I'm not starting down that road because I have things I want to do tonight. Other than go home and watch television."

He vanished into the parking lot, leaving a very confused Clay in his wake.

Mitch let out a big sigh. "Okay, he's definitely got a stick up his butt but, Clay, lay off the mothering."

"What did I do?" Clay grumbled. "Just made one damn comment—"

"You always make one damn comment more than you should. We're all grown-ups now, and you don't need to watch over us like a mother hen."

"You haven't complained about it for a long time," Clay said. "And Len has never complained."

Mitch and Len exchanged glances. While it was a little out of the blue, this was a conversation they should have had long ago. And Len couldn't leave it up to Mitch like he always had before.

He faced Clay straight on. "I don't complain about much."

"That's true." Clay hesitated. "So, does that mean I'm a royal asshole?"

Len give a shrug. "You have your moments. You mean well, but you have a definite opinion about how people should go about things. You're not necessarily wrong, but a guy likes to decide for himself. Troy isn't stupid, and he's not twelve, so give him room and let him make his own mistakes. Knowing he can come to you at any time is more important than you stomping on him to keep him on the straight and narrow."

He turned back to the car he'd offered to work late on, popping open the hood to get started.

Behind him the low sound of clapping broke out. He glanced over his shoulder to see Mitch grinning from ear to ear as he applauded.

"Shut up."

Mitch only grinned harder. "You don't say much, but when you do, *bam*. That was one hefty two-by-four."

Clay looked a little dumbfounded. "Did it really sound like I was stomping on Troy?"

Len paused. Just like he'd had his reasons for growing quiet, he was sure Clay had his for why he'd turned overprotective. "You like all of us to stay safe, and I get that. But you can't shelter us forever."

His brother nodded slowly, as if considering the whole situation from a new perspective. "I don't mean to be an ass."

"Good to know," Mitch taunted. "Keep it that way, because I'd hate to see what life would be like if you were trying."

Clay caught Mitch by the shoulder, and the two of them wrestled briefly until laughter and good-natured brotherly taunting returned.

By the time they got it together and left, Len was happy to have silence surround him. Except that after a few minutes, the place seemed strangely alone. He headed to the sound system and cranked up the music, filling the shop with a heavy beat to distract him from dropping everything to go see what Janey was up to.

Yep, Len would admit it. He was as bad as Clay in some ways, especially when it came to protecting Janey.

He knew she was capable and strong, as demonstrated by how quickly things were progressing around the building site. She worked damn hard, yet when they did other activities she was an enthusiastic participant, and she still found the energy to fool around.

She'd be leaving in a couple months. All he could do was enjoy their time together, and be glad he'd briefly gotten to experience her fire.

The repair job took less mental power and more brute strength, and he ended up stripping off his shirt to wipe the sweat from his brow after crawling out from underneath the chassis. He lowered the wheels to the ground and got ready to do the rest of the tune-up when a low whistle pulled his attention to the door.

"Is this what you do in your after-hours? You got a job as a stripper and you're practicing your moves."

Janey sauntered across the garage floor toward him, her sweet curves hidden under the coverall she wore while working on the house.

"Did you just finish for the day?" he asked.

"I finished three hours ago," she admitted, "but when I couldn't get a hold of you, I decided I might as well do a little more work."

"That was damned stupid. Why didn't you take the evening off?"

She raised a brow. "Because I still had work to do."

Len realized he sounded as overbearing as Clay had earlier in the day. He held up his hands and gave in. "You're right. I meant if you wanted to hit my place and soak in the tub, you're welcome to do that too. Since your tub is still out of commission."

She stepped all the way up, planting a hand on his bare chest. "Now that sounds awfully nice, but I'd like it even better if you were in there with me."

"I don't think my tub's big enough for two people."

She flashed him a dirty smile. "Means we'd have to get really, *really* close."

He didn't mind the sound of that, at least the part about getting close. A glance around the shop brought something more immediate to mind.

Len crooked a finger her direction. "Come here."

She followed without asking any questions, trailing him around the corner to where the project he'd been working on was tucked away. The truck still wasn't ready to take out on the road, but there was one change

Janey hadn't seen yet. He was looking forward to her reaction.

"Oh, it's gorgeous." She ran a hand over the sidewall of the classic truck, carefully stroking the brand-new paint job. She turned back toward him, her smile stretching from ear to ear. "You wild man. You painted her red."

"Just seemed right." The truth was he couldn't picture any other colour after Janey had mentioned it, and if the shiny paint was a little bolder than he would usually have chosen, having that little reminder of her would be worth it.

She pulled open the driver's door and climbed inside, admiring the upholstery and hanging onto the wheel. "You've done a fabulous job. You're good with your hands."

If that wasn't an opening line...

"Promise you'll come driving with me the first night I take her out."

Janey nodded. "I'd love to."

"We can take her to the lookout and park her for a while," Len grabbed Janey by the hand and tugged her out the door.

Her expression grew more interested. "What would we be planning on doing while we were parked?"

"I'm pretty sure we can think of a thing or two."

Janey leaned into him, curling her fingers around the back of his neck and kissing him eagerly.

There was a *thing or two* on his mind right now. He reached down and picked her up, her legs automatically wrapping around his hips as he sauntered toward the back of the truck. Their lips stayed in contact, slow leisurely kisses revving up his system like usual.

He held her with one hand and dropped the tailgate, lowering her carefully to the metal surface.

She smiled at him with eyes full of fire. "Everybody gone home for the day? Your dad's not upstairs in his apartment?"

"Shop is closed. Dad is out with his buddies for his weekly night of pool and bullshit. Unless someone comes back accidentally, it's going to be pretty quiet." He ran his hand down her cheek, resting his fingers loosely on her neck. "Except for the part where I make you scream."

"Oh, really?" She tugged at his belt. "You upping the ante to screaming already?"

"I don't know that it's so much me as you. You're noisy in the sack." He undid the top button of her coverall.

"Noisy? Really?" Her lips pulled into that damn sexy pout.

"I love it," he confessed. "Every moan and whimper."

Her eyes flashed and her chin tilted up. "I can be silent. Can you talk dirty?"

Now there was a challenge he could get behind. He had her buttons undone and was ready to push the material off her shoulders, but he paused. "Just because I don't talk a lot doesn't mean I'm not thinking dirty things."

"So, you gonna tell me them?" The fire in her honey-brown eyes flared hotter.

130

"Hell, yeah. Stand up on the tailgate and take off your clothes."

She scrambled to her feet and let the blue coverall pool around her ankles. Len caught her fingers, giving her something to brace against as she stepped out of the material and kicked it aside. Underneath she was wearing a T-shirt and shorts, both of which came off quickly to be added to the growing pile on top of the coverall.

"You take off your bra," Len ordered. "I get to take off your panties."

Janey reached behind her and undid the snap, catching hold of the bra cups in front and holding them in place with one arm as she shrugged out of the shoulder straps.

"Don't be shy, sweetheart. Show your pretty breasts to me," he demanded, leaning on the tailgate and looking up with heated anticipation.

She let her arms fall away, leaving herself totally exposed to his sight. The full curves of her breasts tugged a heavy sigh of satisfaction from his lips. "So fucking gorgeous."

Janey licked her lips, and it was like a delicious banquet lay before him. Len took a deep breath. He was torn between moving forward or staying right where they were so he could enjoy it for longer.

But first? He'd been given a challenge.

He stared at her chest for another moment, the tips of her nipples tightening as he watched. Len lifted his gaze far enough to stare into her eyes. At the dark pupils growing wider as she looked back.

"I want to pull you close so I can take a bite. Lick you up and down and everywhere until you squirm. When I suck on your nipples and use my teeth, you make this purring sound that gets my cock so hard I don't know how I last long enough to slip inside your pussy. It's like that noise is the starter gun, and everything else that follows is one wicked race of pleasure."

She swallowed hard, and then he didn't see her reaction any further because his gaze dropped to her hips. He caught hold of the side of her underwear, but instead of stripping it off, he ran his hands along the bottom edge, slipping it higher and higher until the soft fabric curled in on itself, riding up between her pussy lips and her ass. "You ever wear thongs?" he asked.

"No. I thought they would be pretty uncomfortable— *Oh*—"

He tugged the fabric back and forth slightly, rubbing over her clit. "Imagine you working all day, something rubbing against you every time you move. You could pretend it was my tongue on your pussy, licking until you squirm. Tasting you and fucking you with my tongue."

"Oh my."

She spread her legs wider, rocking into his touch.

But he was already done, jerking off the scrap of fabric to prepare for the next bit of torment.

"Watch me," he ordered.

He made sure she had her balance before letting her go, then he stripped away his clothes in record time, stepping back into his work boots. His cock rose high and hard, and he covered himself quickly with a condom before turning back.

She had just licked her lips, moisture shining as she breathed heavily. "Am I making any noises now?" she asked. "Because, damn, you should take this show on the road."

"For your eyes only." He reached his hand out. "Come here."

She leaned forward into his arms, her naked body making contact with his, and they both groaned with satisfaction. She clung to him, staring boldly into his eyes.

"I need to fuck you. You ready?" Len asked

"I'm always ready for you."

Len dragged forward the blanket he had in the back of the truck until it draped over the edge of the tailgate, a soft cushioning for her. Then he dropped her onto it, belly down, squatting briefly behind her. His face in line with her sex.

The lips of her labia were wet with moisture. He stroked a finger over the soft surfaces, humming in approval as she squirmed, trying to keep his hand in contact with her. "What a pretty pussy. I changed my mind. I need a taste before I fuck you."

She was sprawled facedown, her butt sticking over the edge of the tailgate. He pushed one leg to the side, exposing her better as he moved in close and licked her from front to back. *All* the way back, pausing for a second over her ass.

A full-body shiver rocked her. "Holy moly, Len. What are you—?"

He licked her again, teasing her clit for longer until she squirmed then moving to the next spot. He couldn't get enough of her, of the way she wiggled under his hands as he held her pinned to the tailgate.

"I'm going to fuck you hard, and I'm going to play with your ass, and you can make all the damn noises you want because it makes me that much hotter."

He played his fingers into her pussy to get them wet before stroking higher to tease the sensitive bundle of nerves at her ass. At the same time he went back to work, lashing his tongue into her core, lapping her clit until she was squirming, gasps and moans and throaty cries escalating as he pressed a finger into her ass up to the first knuckle while he sucked on her clit.

"Oh, God, *yes...*"

She convulsed around him, her muscles tightening down on his fingertip.

He shot to his feet and pressed the head of his cock to her pussy. He slipped in an inch, pulling out slowly once then thrusting all the way forward. A gasp escaped her, and he froze in place, buried deep.

"Oh, it's good, don't stop," Janey begged.

"Hold on tight," he warned.

Another slow withdrawal, waiting with the crown of his cock nestled between her pussy lips. He hesitated, waiting to hear she was ready, listening to her breathing still as she waited in anticipation.

With a tight grip on both her hips, he thrust forward, driving all the way to the root and forcing a cry of pleasure from her lips. And then there was no stopping. He did it again, and again, her legs swaying as they hung toward the ground. Every thrust rocked the back of the truck slightly, both their bodies in intimate contact. His thighs and balls slapping against her with a rhythmic beat. He gripped her hips tighter and hauled her back against him, pleased to hear her moan of approval.

Stars floated in front of his eyes, but he held on to his control, thrusting with one hand on her hip. The other he placed where he'd had it before, using her own moisture to slip his finger back into the tiny passage between her cheeks.

She tightened for a second before relaxing under him. "Yes."

It wasn't a demand, yet she wasn't begging. It was a simple acknowledgment of need. He picked up the same rhythm as his hips, moving deeper on each thrust until he was fucking her with his cock and his finger at the same time.

She shattered; pulsing around him hard enough Len froze in place to enjoy it more. To feel every sensation as she fisted tighter, dragging a response from him sooner than he wanted.

He rocked forward. Two, maybe three more drives before he came. Shooting into the condom and damn near losing his mind in the process.

They both fought for air. Len's hands were shaking as he withdrew his finger and caught her hips. He leaned over and covered her back with his body, both of them slick with sweat as he dropped a kiss between her shoulder blades.

They stayed there, quietly resting for a moment. Nothing but their breathing and the slow buzz of the diagnostic machines in the background.

"You can talk dirty to me anytime you want." Janey sighed happily.

Len chuckled. "You can fuck my brains out anytime you want."

He pulled out and took care of things as she twisted on the spot to face him. He caught her in his arms, their naked skin pressed together a whole different kind of intimate and dirty. She loosely wrapped her legs around his hips, crossing her ankles to keep them there.

Len held her. His heart racing, his mind racing as well. They were good together, like he always figured they would be. As much as he was glad they had this time together, he was worried he'd made a horrid mistake giving in and taking for even this short while.

They *were* good together. And saying goodbye down the road was going to hurt a hell of a lot.

Chapter Ten

LOUD BANGING jerked her away from her task. Janey laid her hammer on the floor and made her way through the house to the back door, wiping her hands on her coveralls and preparing a smile for whoever was waiting for her.

Somehow, she kept it in place as she stared through the glass at Brad Jons. There was no avoiding him now.

He waved a hand, his bright smile flashing as she pulled the screen door open. "You're a tough woman to get a hold of. I figured I could catch you here, though."

"And you did," Janey forced out. "Want to come in?"

He followed her into the kitchen. "I don't want to interrupt you for long, but I needed to talk to you, and..." His smile twisted, no longer looking nearly so cocky. "I wondered if maybe you had the wrong idea about something, and if you've been trying to avoid me because of it."

Janey hesitated. All kinds of possibilities were opened up by that comment, and she wasn't sure which one she dared unwrap. Saying something noncommittal seemed the safest. "Oh, really?"

Brad nodded, glancing around at the renovations in her kitchen with admiration. "I know my uncle has been in contact with you a few times, but let's face it, he's not always upfront about what he's got on his mind."

He could say that again. "What does he have on his mind?" Janey asked.

Brad turned, his dark eyes examining her carefully. "I know you and I are in the same business, but I don't think we're rivals. In fact, I think we should be working together. There are some tasks that are too big for one person alone, plus there are times I get short-notice calls about projects when I'm already committed to another job."

This was about work? "Wow. Yeah, I had no idea you wanted to talk to me about any kind of job."

"Forget my uncle for now. The only reason he's relevant is one of the jobs I took on in the last while is building maintenance for an apartment house he owns. That was kind of the straw that broke the camel's back, because usually it doesn't involve very difficult maintenance, but when something happens, it's mayhem."

Janey was still attempting to figure out exactly what Brad was offering. "Are you asking me to come work for you?"

Brad shook his head, then paused. "I'm not sure exactly what I'm suggesting. I don't know if it would work for us to both maintain our individual businesses, but find a way to coordinate tasks, or if we should join together and set up one business—but that's a pretty big step to dive into. We need to do a lot more talking first."

"There are a lot of things to think about." The biggest of which was she'd intended to leave at the end of summer. But if she didn't have to go away to find the work she needed, it would be worth the work of setting up a deal with Brad.

He held out a business card. "Here's the phone number for my accountant. Give it some thought. See if it's something you'd consider, and if you'd like more information, set up a time that's convenient for you to meet and I'll be there. He said he'd be willing to go over options with us in terms of business arrangements."

She was a little shocked by the speed of the whole thing. "That's a very generous offer. You'd be basically sharing the business connections you've already established."

He smiled, and this time it didn't come across as a warning signal of trying to take advantage of her—just an honest expression of his pleasure, and a little tired around the edges. "See, there's a difference between being thoughtful and saving my own ass. No good in me having an established business if I can't satisfy my customers. Pretty soon those customers would be looking for other help. I prefer to keep them happy, and if that means bringing in a partner, that's a better idea than screwing up what I've already worked so hard for."

After that, Janey ended up giving him a tour of the entire house, Brad making appropriately enthusiastic comments about the changes she'd made.

By the time he left, her mind was in a whirl. This changed everything, maybe.

Co-owning a business had never been her intention, so it was a change of mindset she still had to work through. But there was so much potential in the idea, not the least of which meant she could stay in town. Close by her friends and everything she'd grown to appreciate.

Including, if she was honest, Len.

She dove into work for a couple of hours more before heading over to Katy's house for lunch.

Her friend greeted her happily, laying little Tanner back in his car seat and lifting a finger to her lips. "Let me put him back in his room."

Janey stirred the soup on the stove and grabbed the fixings for sandwiches. She had everything on the table by the time Katy returned.

"Well, that's nice. I invite you for lunch and you do all the work."

Janey blew a raspberry. "Hardly. You had most of it done." She looked her friend over. "How'd you sleep last night?"

Katy wiggled her fingers. "I'm starting to get used to the mom thing. Waking in the middle of the night isn't my favourite, but at least he's not kicking my bladder anymore."

They both sat and started on the food. "You're going back to work at the garage sometime soon?" Janey asked.

Her friend nodded. "I can bring Tanner with me, or I can bring paperwork home and do it here." She grinned. "One good thing about a family business, I guess. None of my brothers will object to having their nephew on the worksite, as long as he's not in the way."

"You're going to have a mini grease monkey on your hands before you know it."

Katy didn't look at all upset. "I'm so happy," she confessed.

Janey paused in the middle of scooping another spoonful of soup. "What brought that on?"

"If you'd told me a year ago what my life would be like now, I would've called bullshit." Katy gestured around the house. "I know a lot of the trappings look the same, but the two big additions in my life, Gage and Tanner, make everything different."

"Not to mention the accident, the amnesia, the whacked-out ex-boyfriend—" Janey stopped as Katy slapped up a hand. "What? You had all those things happen over the last year as well."

All she got was a slow shake of the head from her friend. "Those aren't what come to mind at all. It's like, I know they're there, and I can't deny them because in some cases, one thing led to another, but the end result is I have so much in my life to be thankful for."

Janey eyed her cautiously. "Are you pregnant? You're like, really hormonal or something."

A burst of laughter greeted her from across the table "Of course I'm not." Katy sobered up a bit and looked thoughtful. "I don't think so. Oh, God, I can't be..."

It was Janey's turn to laugh. "Better you than me. You have the rug-rats. I'm happy to be Auntie Janey to them all."

Katy made a face. "You're mean. And I'm not pregnant."

They talked more, but Janey held back from saying anything about the possible job change.

Talk about a switch in situation. When she was done her renovations she was supposed to be off to Calgary. That's what her parents thought, and her brother and sister. All her plans were aimed in that direction.

Yet, was it what she should do?

She paused in her work later that day, standing in the dining room at the house. Staring out the back window into the yard as Katy's words echoed through her brain.

A year from that moment, where would she be? Would she be somewhere brand new? No longer seeing all of the familiar things, the familiar faces. Not being there as Katy's kids grew up.

It was a wide-open question mark that lay before her, and now suddenly with Brad's offer, there might be two roads she could choose to walk.

LEN PUSHED open the door of Traders Pub, standing aside to let Janey enter ahead of him. A rush of music and heat wrapped around them with a sensual tease as he followed her into the crowded room. The dance-floor side of the pub was filled to capacity, and he wondered if they should try the other side, where there were pool tables and places to sit quietly.

Janey? Had no problem with how busy it was. She waded forward, keeping a tight grip on his hand as she smiled and nodded at everyone they passed.

"You want to sit with your family?" Janey asked, leaning back against his chest as she spoke. "Oh. Forget that. It looks like we've got a Thompson-Coleman free-for-all happening."

He slipped an arm around her, happy as hell he had the privilege to touch her whenever he wanted. "Right. Mitch mentioned something. Birthday for one of the Colemans. Anna figured things might get rowdy."

She laughed, squeezing his fingers briefly before tugging him with her as she threaded her way through the crowd. "Always nice when the cop in the family is on top of these things."

The far corner of the pub had been taken over, familiar faces all around them.

She threw herself into the arms of a dark-haired woman who hugged her tightly. Over Janey's shoulder, Tamara Coleman offered Len a wink then pulled him and Janey into the party.

Around one of the standing-room-only tables, the surface littered with shot glasses and beer bottles, a pack of the Coleman family was gathered. The youngest, Raphael, wore a tolerant smile as one of his cousins propped a tiara on his cowboy hat.

Len reached through the mob to offer his hand. "Another year older."

"But not any wiser," some joker shouted in the background.

Rafe shouted back. "I don't have to get any wiser to be smarter than the lot of you."

A collective *ooooh* echoed from his family.

In the midst of the laughter, Janey slipped in and gave the birthday boy a hug. "You're already cuter than the rest of them, as well," she teased.

Rafe snuck his arm around Janey's waist. "Thanks, darling. So, do I get a birthday dance with you?" He flicked his glance up at Len for a split second before flashing her a cheeky smile. "Something slow..."

Damn brat. "She's taken."

All attention turned on Len, and he didn't give a shit.

Janey raised one brow. "Does this mean *we're* going to dance? Really? Like—actual dancing?"

"Shut up," Len muttered softly as Janey offered him a giggle, covering her mouth with her hand.

Len led her away from the chuckling crowd, found them space on the crowded dance floor and pulled her tight up against his body.

She locked her fingers together behind his neck, settling in intimately with the front of her body in complete contact with his. "Well, now, Len Thompson. It appears you aren't allergic to the dance floor anymore."

He slipped a hand to the center her back and pulled her even tighter against him, leaning over to brush his lips past her ear. "You know why I never danced with you before?"

"Hmmm?"

He rocked their hips together, and the way he instantly reacted to having her in his arms had to be abundantly clear. "No way I was going anywhere near you when I couldn't take what I wanted so badly."

Her eyes flashed. Her tongue slipped out and did a slow roll over her lips, leaving them shining with moisture. Len kissed her briefly, pulling back before he could be tempted to get any dirtier.

But there was nothing saying he couldn't tell her some of the things he wanted to do. He put his lips back where he could speak quietly and not be overheard, even by those swaying together close around them.

"I've got your breasts pressed to me. I can feel how hot you are. If I grabbed your hips and lifted you, I could rub your pussy against my cock until both—"

"Len. Stop it." In spite of the heat, Janey shivered. "God. I can picture it."

She rubbed against him, and the touch wasn't nearly enough to ease the aching pressure in his cock. "So can I."

Janey caught him by the front of his shirt. "What happened to my shy, quiet man?"

Len shrugged. "I'm still quiet. Don't say much."

"No," she agreed. "But what you do say is damn filthy."

She fanned a hand in front of her face for a second, and he laughed, moving her into a less intimate position as the music changed and the tempo picked up.

As long as she was somewhere in his arms, he didn't mind the dancing bit.

Janey finally begged off. "I need to hit the washroom."

She wiggled away from him, her fingers trailing out of his hand as she flashed him a mischievous smile. "Grab me a drink?"

He nodded, watching her ass for as long as he possibly could until it vanished around the corner.

After picking up a couple of drinks, he found a space between a couple of the guys. Len halfheartedly listened to their discussion, but he was more interested in watching for her to come back

"You're certainly obsessed," Trevor teased. One of Anna's brothers, he'd spent more time around the Thompson boys then a lot of the Coleman clan. "When are you going to give the rest of us a chance to dance with her?"

A hot flash of jealousy clicked through Len, and he shoved it away as quickly as he could. "Up to Janey."

Trevor shook his head. "I don't think so. I mean, maybe you know that's a safe thing to say because she's only got eyes for you, like always."

Satisfaction rolled hard, and Len didn't even try to hide it. "Good."

The other man laughed. "Obsessed, *and* possessive. Yeah, you're a Thompson."

"You mean he's a guy." Janey slipped into the conversation as she wormed her way under his arm and picked up her drink. She took a long swallow before smiling at him. "Most guys have trouble moving past the 'it's mine' stage of the playground. Especially when it comes to women."

She gave him a wink and turned to Trevor to ask him about something on the ranch. They chatted for a bit while Len listened. He was more focused on Janey being pressed against him, all soft and warm. Moving into his touch as he stroked her arm.

All of it got him hotter by the minute. And every time she glanced up, it was obvious he wasn't the only one feeling the heat.

The music volume rose, and she hauled him onto the dance floor, the front buttons of her shirt now undone to a perilous level. From the expression in her eyes, she knew she was playing with fire.

Long before closing, Len was done. He waited until she'd paused during a conversation with her friends before leaning down and whispering in her ear, "Let's go."

What he had in mind must have been on hers as well. She turned to Shannon and Liz. "Talk to you later."

Feminine laughter followed as he damn near manhandled her out the door.

In front of him, Janey twirled, taunting him as she swayed her hips from side to side. "You're a good dancer,

Len Thompson. I've been wondering about your moves for a long time."

"You gonna get another dose of my moves damn soon," he offered. Sweeping her off the ground and into his embrace as he strode through the parking lot.

She locked her arms around his neck, tossing him a sultry look. "Well, that sounds mighty fine. Where are we going to do this...dancing?"

There were too many possibilities, and most of them were too far away.

Janey waggled her brows. "Ooh, I recognize that expression. Like a puppy dog whose favourite toy has been taken away."

Len laughed. "So, I'm a dog now?"

"Only if you insist." She tilted her head towards his truck. "Get in. Let me drive."

He didn't argue, even though he was curious as all get out. He found his seat gingerly, desperate to find more room for his cock.

When she pulled into the back alley, and then into the parking spot behind her house, he was ready to pick her up bodily and run inside.

Only she stopped him in his tracks. "Open your pants," she ordered.

He paused long enough to see her reach under her skirt and pull off her panties. "Jeez, Janey."

In a flash, she was on her knees, kneeling on the bench seat beside him. "Hurry up. You got me so damn hot on the dance floor."

Then she was kissing him, her lips hot against his neck, rubbing her breasts against his torso as he scrambled to release his cock. He was totally on board with the speed they were going, except there was something…

"Condom." Thank God his brain wasn't completely gone.

"Shit." Janey dove for her purse, reaching in then throwing it back on the floor. Somehow she had a condom package open and her soft hands rolling the latex down before he had time to breathe a word of protest.

She caught hold of his face, her knees straddling his hips. "I need you to fuck me now."

She accompanied her words with the full-body stroke over his length, the hot moisture of her pussy like a GPS signal calling him home. The next thing he knew she was sinking over him, surrounding him with her tight warmth. "God damn."

They were sitting in the dark, twenty feet from her back door, their bodies intimately connected while mostly dressed. It was the hottest damn thing Len had ever experienced.

He caught hold of her chin and kissed her, pressing a hand to the curve of her lower back and over her ass. Thrusting with his hips as he mimicked the motion with his tongue into her mouth. Janey made a noise that brought his blood to a boil, and he lost it. Pounding upward, her breasts jiggling against his body as his name escaped her in a long, breathless cry.

Somehow he got a hand between them and added pressure to her clit. Her head fell back, and he scraped his teeth along her neck, setting a bite at the soft curve where her neck and shoulder met.

The sweat from her body lit his taste buds like firecrackers, all the dancing they'd done earlier combining together with the sexual dance now, and she rocked hard, breaking apart in his arms.

He thrust once more before joining her.

"*Janey…*"

The truck, that must've been bouncing, settled into quiet as they worked to catch their breath. Both of them looked thoroughly debauched, their clothing out of sorts.

Janey lifted her satisfied gaze to his and licked her lips. "Holy fuck. When you said you had the moves, you weren't lying."

The laughter that seemed to arrive all too easily around her was back. Len felt no shame in cuddling her close. She nestled against him, nuzzling his neck, stroking her fingers through his hair. Len stared through the front window at the house and tried not to think about everything that would change in the future.

Right here, right now, he was a happy man.

Chapter Eleven

JANEY STOOD, stretching her back after working on the baseboards.

The list of things that needed to be finished around the house was getting shorter, and she was damn proud of everything she'd accomplished.

Janey glanced across the room at Len, mentally adjusting that last statement. She had done a lot, but she had to admit over the summer Len had stepped in often to help her with tasks. If he hadn't done as much, no way she would be at this point.

"That's the last baseboard," Len offered. "What's next, boss?"

"I think it's quitting time. And I don't know if you should call me boss or master. I'm paying you slave wages."

Len smiled as he joined her. "I don't mind lending a hand."

She grabbed a couple of drinks from the fridge and gestured to the deck. "Come on. Let's sit and rest for a while."

The deck had been completed and stained, and Katy had lent her a set of lawn chairs so they had somewhere to sit while taking a break.

Janey twisted off the top and handed the beer to him. "I think I got about a week's work at the outside to get everything done."

He took a long drink, looking steadily into the backyard. He nodded but didn't say anything.

She hesitated. He wasn't a big talker, she knew that. And while they were working together, it never bothered her. Then it seemed she understood his silence was to avoid blabbing about nothing.

At times like this? It was different. Something she couldn't quite define, but the silence sat uneasy and uncomfortable. And no matter how much she enjoyed his dirty talk in bed, and the romping between the sheets, she was sure something was wrong.

It really was time to bring up the business idea she'd been offered. She'd talked to Katy about it, but sworn her friend to secrecy until she got a chance to consider the options. But more was at stake than simply a job, and if there was one thing she admired about Len, it was how good he was at seeing the big picture.

Maybe because he wasn't spending all his time talking, he got more of a chance to listen. She could use a little bit of his rock-solid consideration to add to her pros-and-cons list.

"Len. Can I ask you something?"

He stiffened.

The unexpected reaction was subtle, but it was there.

What the hell? She was about to ask him what was wrong when a loud *hello* rang out from the back gate.

"I finally caught you at the right time." Mr. Jons stepped across the yard, his gaze darting from side to side as he checked out everything. "Looks fabulous. You've done a great job of getting the place up to date."

Beside her, Len relaxed as if grateful for the interruption.

Damn the timing. Janey forced herself to be polite. "Thank you."

Jons stopped at the edge of the decking, stomping his way up the stairs as if checking if they were strong enough. "Yes, it looks as if you've done a *very* good job."

"You'll have to tell my parents that." It was too tempting to resist.

"I have been," Jons admitted. "Just last weekend I was talking to them and said as far as I was concerned, you've done more than was necessary. No lipstick on a pig here."

A rude noise escaped Len that he attempted to cover with a cough.

Jons gave him a brief glance then focused back on Janey. "Are you ready to list her?"

"Soon," Janey admitted.

Jons nodded. "Well. There's nothing saying you have to, but I really hope you'll consider using me as your realtor. I have some people I think might be interested. No guarantees, but I might be able to get you a quick turnaround. Not easy in this current housing market."

Okay. Janey owed Shannon a drink for not believing the man simply wanted her business. Her imagination had her seeing conspiracies when there were none.

Or had it been her guilt at not following the family path?

She smiled. Funny how now that she was more confident in her abilities and decision making, her parents' supposed judgment, and Marty Jons', didn't bother her as much.

He was one of the top-ranked realtors in the community, so as long as he wasn't up to any funny business, Janey had no objections with using his company. "I'll give it some thought."

Jons tilted his head toward the house. "I don't want to interrupt your drink, but do you mind if I take a look inside?"

Len got to his feet. "I have to run anyway. Janey, call me later?"

"You don't have to go," she objected.

"Call me," he said. "I need to get caught up on some things at home."

He put his half-drunk beer down on the side table and then damn near sprinted off the deck, headed around the corner before she could even say goodbye.

From inside the house, Jons offered a whistle of admiration. "Is this new hardwood?"

She had to follow him to answer a million questions, and all the while she had a million more pop into her head, most concerning her future.

Maybe the house was ready to sell, but she wasn't ready to leave. Not after the summer and the time she'd gotten to enjoy with Len. And that wasn't even counting how much she would miss her other friends.

When she'd planned to move to Calgary, it had been a necessity for work. She still might have to do it, at least for a short time, but maybe there was a way around that. If the situation with Brad worked out, she wouldn't have to leave at all.

It was so tempting, and so potentially right. She was damn near giddy as she answered Jons and considered her future.

Maybe she wouldn't discuss it with Len yet. He obviously had something on his mind, plus she needed to make sure she was doing this for the right reasons, i.e., just because she'd been having an amazing time with the man didn't mean she should base her future decisions around him.

Making a huge change in plans, like where to work and where to live—she needed to base those decisions on what she really wanted. It had to come from her heart.

Even as the little voice inside her informed her Len Thompson *was* a part of her heart...

HE'D ESCAPED, thankful in a way for the interruption. It had stopped him from coming too close to once again blurting out a request for Janey to change her mind and not sell the house.

He had no right to be dictating things to her. Being with her had become an addiction.

Heading home was out of the question—he didn't want to see any signs of her right now, and in subtle ways, she was everywhere. The shampoo she'd bought and left in the shower, the spare shoes she'd lined up at the front door next to his.

He turned into the shop intending to finish some extra work when he spotted a light on in his dad's apartment over the garage. Keith Thompson had moved into the place once Katy was old enough to live in the family home on her own.

Len paused. He'd never given it much thought before, how his dad chose to live in a cramped, one-bedroom space right over the shop instead of remaining in the house across the yard where the entire family had grown up—

His feet moved involuntarily toward the stairwell, and he found himself knocking on the door. There was no answer, but a low pulse of music carried through the wood, so Len opened the door cautiously and made his way inside.

"Dad?"

His father turned from the window, a tortured expression on his face and sorrow in his eyes. He didn't answer, just shuffled across the room to settle in his chair. The single light in the room glowed down on the framed picture of Len's mom and dad on their wedding day. Bright faces shining. Hope and love so clearly visible.

Shit. This could get rough.

A nearly empty bottle of whiskey sat next to the chair, and his dad tipped a little more into his glass, hands shaking as he raised the tumbler toward the picture.

"Meg said yes. On this day, all those years ago. I thought for sure she was smarter than that—thought she would tease me for a little longer before she agreed we should get married. I mean, I was this dumb hick grease-monkey, and she was so smart and beautiful, and she could have had anyone she wanted."

"Of course she said yes. You were in love." Len gingerly lowered himself into the chair opposite his father and prepared to babysit for a while—the man was drunk enough to need to be watched. "I can't believe you remember the anniversary of the day you proposed."

Keith sighed. "I remember it all, far too much, because memories are all I've got left."

His voice cracked for a second, and Len swallowed hard.

Silence reigned before his dad started talking. Stories about courting Len's mom. Dances and parties, and walks down country lanes. Len sat and listened. He wasn't quite sure what to do with his hands as the bands around his heart tightened more with every moment of painful remembrance.

And then it happened. His father strolled straight into the fire, hauling Len with him. "I don't know if I've ever said thank you."

Len stiffened in his chair, staring across at his father as a sense of dread rushed in to fill his soul. "For what?"

Keith stared at the glass in his hand as if it held the secrets of the universe. "I know what you did. More than you should've had to at your age."

Utter dismay washed over Len, a sense of nausea rising. "What are you talking about?"

"The night your mom died." Keith took a long drink, staring out the window at the clouds gathered like dark omens over the mountains. He shook his head. "I couldn't do it. I just couldn't."

Len's body shook as he waited, careful not to say anything out of place. Careful not to give any opening or assume what his father was talking about even as his emotions whirled in turmoil.

It was the same sense of fear and self-loathing he'd lived with for years as a teenager. The way his heart would stop beating every time the police would walk by, or someone paused and looked at him for too long.

He'd gotten past that, he'd thought. Past the nausea and the pain. But it was right back strong as the day it had first slashed him to the heart.

Keith shook his head, his lined face tight with emotion. His voice breaking as he spoke. "I miss her so damn much. Why'd she have to die, Len? Why'd she have to go and leave me without my heart?"

"She didn't want to, Dad." Len stared across at his father, a strong man broken by an event that had happened more than ten years earlier. And like back then, Len did what he could to bring peace. "She fought, she fought hard."

"Fuck cancer. Stole the heart of our family. Stole my heart until I'm nothing left but a walking husk. If I could change places with her, I would, in a second."

His father put his face in his hands and the tears began to fall.

Len wiped his eyes, fighting to stay in control. There was nothing he could say. Just like there'd been nothing he could do so long ago, nothing except be there and offer a warm body in the room.

He didn't know the words, and he didn't know how to cut out his father's pain like they'd tried to cut the cancer from his mother's body.

In the end, both were killers.

His mother hadn't lasted past that summer. His father had never been the same, and once again a part inside of Len grew cold with fear and frustration.

He crossed the room and wrapped an arm around his father's shoulders. The same way he'd done when his mom had died. Sobs wracked Keith's body, and Len sat there, trying to offer *something* to bring back his father from the dark pit of despair.

In that moment Len's resolve stiffened. The pleasure and joy he'd found over the summer in Janey's presence was temporary and fleeting, and he needed to cut loose as soon as possible.

Because that's all his soul could take.

Chapter Twelve

HER FINGERS were numb from clutching the phone so tight. "No way. You're serious?"

Mr. Jons chuckled. "I joke about many things, but house sales are not one of them. Congratulations. If everything works out, you'll be the proud ex-owner of your place by the end of the month."

Shock and joy danced together all the way to her feet until Janey couldn't keep still. She bounced down the hallway. "I thought you said the market was slow these days. We only listed the house last weekend, and I didn't expect any serious offers for a few days if we were lucky."

"Doesn't take luck when it's a great house and someone's looking. They pretty much accepted your terms. I'll bring by the paperwork to show you what's happening, and we'll take it from there."

"You'll come here? Or do you want me to come to your office. I can come to your office." She could *fly* to his office she was so full of adrenaline.

Jons laughed. "You're going to be out of a place to sleep. Now you really need to tell me if you want to consider renting that apartment."

Janey resisted answering his question, because she and Brad hadn't finished working out the details, but there was a good chance she *would* need to find a place to rent. "I'll be at the office in a few minutes."

As excited as she was, she resisted calling Len.

Something strange was going on with him. At first she'd thought it was her imagination, or an exhausted assumption on her part. The final week of getting the house finished had turned into a few near-twenty-four-hour workdays. Len had still come around and helped her, but they'd been swamped at the garage as well, so their moments together had been few and far between. They hadn't once had sex during that time, either, which was kind of like going from a feast to a famine. Pretty much, they'd talked a few times, and once they'd gotten together to sit quietly on the deck.

Janey had fallen asleep in his arms and discovered herself alone in her bed hours later.

But everything, as confusing and unsettling as it was, could be pushed behind her now. There was no more rush, there were no more reasons they couldn't go back to having a good time together, and maybe more.

She laughed with relief as she hopped into her truck, forcing herself to stay under the speed limit all the way to the realtor's office. She couldn't resist grabbing her phone and calling Katy, though.

"I got an offer, and he says it's really good, and I'm going to the office to see if I've actually sold the house."

Katy squealed loud enough to satisfy Janey. "That is so awesome. Do you know who bought it? Do you know when they'd be moving? Oh man, you haven't figured out where you're going to live yet. What you gonna do with your stuff? If you need somewhere to store it, you can stick it in my garage, or I bet there's room down at the shop—"

"Let's wait until things are actually in place before we worry about where my boxes have to go," Janey warned. "But, yes, I am *so* excited. And I don't know what's coming next, but it's like doors are opening."

"This is when I start singing 'The Sound of Music' to annoy you, right?"

Janey didn't think anything could ever annoy her again. "You can 'Do-Re-Mi' anytime you want. I'm at the office, I'll call you soon as I find out the rest of the news."

"Congratulations, though. You worked really hard, and I'm so glad it's paid off."

A cloud of warmth surrounded her as Janey floated into the office, the little bell over the door buzzing softly. Mr. Jons beckoned her from the back, and she walked straight in and sat down at the broad boardroom table.

"The offer is for your asking price, which is less uncommon than you'd think," Mr. Jons shared. "The purchaser has financing in place with the bank, so all they need is your agreement with the price."

"That's it?" Janey hesitated. "There's no house inspection as a condition?"

Mr. Jons shrugged. "I guess they trust your building ability. No inspection, as is, and a two-week possession date."

It was a dream offer. Janey shook her head. "Well, I don't want to complain about the basket of gold I'm being offered. Is it someone from out of town who's looking to move in so quickly?"

Mr. Jons flipped through the papers in his hand to where the information was, laying the forms in front of her. "No, local fellow. You know him."

Janey spotted the name on the papers the same moment Mr. Jons announced *Len Thompson*. The warmth and buzz of excitement inside her changed to confusion. "Len put the offer in on my house?"

"Yes. Obviously knows it's a high-quality location, and really, a great deal."

Janey wasn't sure what to say anymore. "Len Thompson wants to buy my house."

The information stuck in her brain like a broken cog clicking over again and again, and never moving forward. She couldn't imagine why this was happening.

Len buying a house wasn't out of the question. The place was a little bigger than a single guy needed, but it would be quieter than his apartment, and...

She didn't want to make any assumptions, but damn her brain for going down paths it shouldn't. What if he wasn't planning on having the house to himself? What if there was someone else he wanted in the house with him?

She swallowed hard. "Can I have a bit of time to think about this?" she asked.

Mr. Jons looked shocked. "Of course, if you need it, but..." He frowned, looking her over more carefully. "Are you okay? I thought you'd be happy."

"Oh, I am," she reassured him. "I mean, I'm happy, but I'm a little confused. How long do we have to answer the offer?"

"Twenty-four hours." Jons pulled the papers towards himself. "There's no problem, I don't mind explaining if you have questions, or finding out some more details. You can counteroffer with anything, you just need to let me know."

Janey shoved her chair back and stumbled from the table, making it to the hallway with unsteady feet. "I've got your card, and I'll give you a call as soon as I can."

She turned and all but raced from the office, madly trying to figure out exactly what had just happened.

Len Thompson had bought her house.

Was he trying to tell her something in his silent *never really saying the words but saying a whole hell of a lot without them* kind of way? Because she couldn't think of why he would need a house unless...

Unless he wanted her with him?

Was this why his behavior had been so strange over the past couple weeks? She sat behind the wheel of her truck and stared unseeingly at the traffic going past.

Of all the awkward, potentially exciting, potentially horrifying situations. She was frozen. There was no good way to go about the next steps without coming off as either a presumptuous fool or holding back the excitement she should be enjoying.

So.

No use in waiting any longer. She might as well go for the gusto and find out exactly what the heck was going on.

Facing him down in the garage seemed to add another layer of risk, but at least she knew she could find him there. Walking through the front door and looking out into the familiar confines of the shop helped settle her bouncing nerves.

The scents of gas and oil filled her head, the metallic ring in her ears of tools being used—both were familiar and calming. She'd played in this area when she and Katy were younger. And while the butterflies didn't totally stop dancing on her nerves, at least she didn't feel quite so nauseous anymore.

She snuck past Keith Thompson, the man waving distractedly at her as he stood at the front desk dealing with a customer.

Slipping in through the staff door meant the warning buzzer didn't go off, so all the guys were still working, eyes turned away from her.

That gave her a chance to find Len and watch him for a while. He was doing bodywork on the side panel of a car, his arm moving in a rhythmic motion as he pounded out a dent. All of his attention focused downward, thick gloves on his hands. His biceps flexing with every move.

Totally focused on the project. She knew what it was like to have that intensity turned on her, and the thought made her smile. She had nothing to fear. It was silly to be nervous.

Janey took a deep breath and stepped into her future.

"Heads up," she called as she closed in on him. "You're going to put Thor out of a job."

Len paused, straightening and offering her a brief nod. "Hey. I didn't expect to see you here."

"Well, now that the house is done, I'm living a life of leisure," she teased, her confidence shaking slightly as the word *house* reminded her why she was there.

Len put down the mallet, glancing briefly around the room. "You want to talk?"

She didn't know what to do with her hands. He hadn't pulled her in for a kiss, and she wasn't about to force herself on him. Something awkward hovered between them, but she wasn't sure how much of that was her fault for the assumed thoughts in her brain.

She tilted her head toward the yard door. "Can we go outside?"

He nodded, hesitating for a second before he held out his hand. Janey took it gratefully, wrapping her fingers around his. Savouring the warmth as he guided her from the room and into the late-summer sunshine.

Go for broke. It was the only way, kind of like pulling a loose tooth and getting it over with. "I talked to my realtor…"

It was the perfect opening as far as she was concerned, but again, he didn't do anything more than nod.

Discomfort rose. "Len. You bought my house."

He wasn't frowning or anything, but he didn't offer her a secretive glance or anything to reassure her she wasn't going nuts. Instead, he turned and paced into the yard, moving away as he lifted his face towards the sun.

He turned back slowly. "It's a good house."

She shook her head. "But, I don't get it. You bought my house."

He nodded. Didn't say anything else. Didn't offer any reason why, didn't do something over-the-top crazy-in-love like drop to one knee and propose.

And when he did speak, it was to shatter all of the fledgling dreams she'd begun to risk.

"I guess you'll be off to Calgary as soon as possible."

Pain stuttered across her nerves. She opened then closed her mouth a couple of times, looking for the right answer.

At the same time a trickle of heat ignited deep inside her belly. "Sounds as if you're eager to get rid of me," Janey observed.

Len shrugged. "I know you've got things to do, and the fall is a decent time to find a job. Better sooner than later."

Oh, God. He was serious.

Janey wrapped her arms around herself in self-defense, raising a wall between her and the man she'd thought she was falling in love with.

In spite of the sun beating down on them, she was cold. An icy layer enveloped her, driving spikes into her heart. "I guess you're right. There's not much reason for me to stick around here anymore. Now that the house is sold, and all."

"If you need help loading your truck for the move, let me know."

She wasn't sure how it was possible to be as broken inside and still feel such rising anger. "You're not just eager to get rid of me, you're as good as shoving me out the door."

For the first time Len's expression changed. He looked surprised, shocked even. "Are you mad at me?"

A tortured sound escaped her lips. "Are you kidding me? You have no idea what this sounds like from my side. It's as if you can't wait for me to get out of town."

"I thought—"

"I don't think you really have," Janey snapped, all of her frustrations exploding as she lost control. "Thinking would require that you actually gave a damn, and it's obvious you don't."

His face tightened. "That's not true."

"Oh, really? And I would know this how? Because everything you've done and everything you've said right now proves you care?" Janey swallowed hard. "You know, there are times when I was pretty sure you and I had something special happening. And I'm not talking about the sex, I'm talking about something in here."

She pressed a hand over her chest where it felt as if her heart had shattered and only sheer willpower was keeping it together.

"I care about you," Len insisted.

She shook her head, then reluctantly gave a single nod. "Okay. I will accept you care about me as much as you're willing. But you know what I just realized? It's not enough."

His expression darkened, his gaze boring into her.

He wanted her out of town? Hell, he wanted their entire relationship to be over. Loaded into the back of her truck and driving away down the highway.

Tough shit for him.

Janey lifted her chin. "You've been someone special in my life for a long time, and I thought this summer meant something to us both. But I'm worth someone who wants me passionately, not only in the sack, but in every single thing we do. Someone who shows me how much I mean to them all the time. And that doesn't need fancy presents, or fancy words, Len. It doesn't require you to be someone you aren't."

She stepped toward him, closing the distance as he stood his ground. She stared up at him. At the wall he'd erected between them for some reason.

"But when you refuse to be yourself. When you hide what's important to you—what hurts you, what makes you happy—all those things are part of you, and when you refuse to share those things with me, it shows you don't feel the same way about me I thought I was feeling about you."

He didn't answer, and that in itself told her so much.

"I deserve it all. I deserve all of you, and if you can't give that to me, then it's good I found out now. I don't want to be around you every day for the rest of my life knowing I need more, and that you have it in you, yet you refuse to give it to me."

She turned on her heel and headed toward the shop, moving quickly in spite of the tears filling her eyes. At her back, there was nothing but silence. Like a gravestone being raised over the relationship she'd hoped for.

It was dead before it truly had a chance to live.

Chapter Thirteen

THE COMPLETE coldness in her eyes near the end was what made it real. Up until that moment, Len had been holding himself together. His soul hurt, but it hurt less now than it would down the road.

Or at least that's what he told himself as she walked away. As she walked away and took his fucking heart with her. He refused to give in to the need screaming through him to chase her down and tell her it was all a huge mistake.

Instead he turned and went back to his job, thankful for the monotony of the task because he wasn't thinking very hard at that moment. He was clinging to control, doubting his decision, but knowing in the end it was the right thing for them both.

Only today there was no joy in the banter with his brothers. No joy in being surrounded by his family.

Len watched carefully as his father drifted through the day, a touch more lively than the previous week. One of his greatest fears was that at some point his father would give in to the memories and never come back. That he'd be desperate enough to do *anything* to get rid of the pain he carried every day.

Len could only watch and hope, and do everything he damn well could to avoid the same fate.

Signing the final papers for the house purchase a couple days later didn't provide the kind of relief he'd expected. Maybe once Janey was out of town, he'd be able to get on with his life, and she'd find things to do, and new people to help her be happy in her new situation.

It was for the best even as staying away from her killed him.

His little sister, though, had a few choice words for him as she barged through his apartment door and raced into his face. "Have you gone out of your damn mind? What the hell did you do to Janey?"

"Nothing."

Katy narrowed her eyes. "So in the past three days, you haven't seen her?"

Len shook his head.

"Oh, for heaven's sake. You're not only an idiot, you're a coward."

He frowned. "I bought her house. The housing market is slow, and she needed to get to Calgary so she could get on with her life."

Katy's jaw fell open, and she seemed to hesitate for a moment, her gaze darting around the room as she floundered for words. "I stand corrected. You're an idiot, a coward, and *clueless*."

He went back to packing the box in front of him. She could insult him all she wanted, and the words wouldn't change a thing. It wouldn't bring Janey back into his life, and the sooner he got over that dream, the easier the weight in his heart would be to carry.

Unfortunately, his little sister was a bit of a terrier. She shuffled up beside him and hopped on the counter so she could glare at him easier. "Let me get this straight. You bought her house so that she could leave Rocky Mountain House quicker."

He nodded.

Her eyes damn near rolled back in her head. "I wish smacking you would knock some sense into that thick skull of yours." She leaned forward and spoke slowly. "Janey isn't leaving."

A sick sensation grew in his gut. "What are you talking about?"

His little sister spoke slowly, as if giving time for the words to sink in. "She found a job in town. The only reason she was going to Calgary was for work, and now that she's got something figured out here, she's staying."

Len didn't feel very steady on his feet for a moment, clutching the counter to keep himself upright. "Shit."

"Shit is right." Katy folded her arms over her chest. "Len, you're the only big brother who never tormented me, so I'm going to hope for the best here and assume you don't realize exactly how cruel what you've done is."

"I'm clueless," he confessed, echoing her words.

She held up a hand and ticked off fingers. "You spent the summer with Janey, and I'd swear the two of you got along like nobody's business. You're good together, Len. All of a sudden, out of the blue, you buy her house. The place you know she loves and was fixing up to sell only because she couldn't afford to stay in it herself, but it's home to her like nowhere else has ever been. And then *you* buy it.

"My first assumption is you have some alternative motive like...oh, I don't know. How about like you actually want her to move in with you, and that—"

Len swore. "Oh fuck. Is that what Janey thought?"

"I don't know because other than telling me the bare bones of what happened the other day, my best friend hasn't said much more than two words in a row—most of the time which are 'stupid bastard', by the way. That's all wrong as well, because Janey being a Sphinx about anything means she's hurting bad. But there being some grand secret plans for the two of you? That was the first thing *I* thought when I heard you'd bought the house. Chances are the thought must've crossed her mind as well."

The sick sensation in his gut only got stronger. Especially as Katy continued on her rampage, driving the spike deeper.

"Then, instead of doing something cheesy but romantic like proposing, or at least asking her to set up a love nest with you, you get all excited about how fast she'll be out of your hair."

"It wasn't like that," Len protested. It hadn't been like that at all.

"Hey, I'm telling it like I see it. You can have any delusions on the matter all you want, but when it comes down to it, sure looks a lot like you're shoving her out the door then locking it behind her." Katy dropped her arms and her expression softened. "If that's not what you intended, you fucked up big time. But Janey has a huge heart, and if you apologize, I bet she'd forgive you and you could start again."

A new start was what he wanted so badly, because the thought of leaving her, the realization that he'd *hurt* her...

Fear flared inside, like a wind fanning the banked coals from years earlier. His father's hopelessness, the agony of loss. It was too real.

Maybe he and Janey wanted each other now, but some time in the future he'd lose her—there was no getting around that truth. Plus, what she'd shouted at him the other day was real. He'd kept a part of himself from her, and he didn't think he could ever take down the walls he'd constructed to guard his soul. He'd always be holding back, and she deserved everything.

Janey does damn good renovations.

The temptation was there whispering in his ear, but the sorrows from years earlier were too much to push aside. No matter how much he wanted to change his path, he couldn't. As much as they were hurting right now, if they went forward they could get over it.

The process would be a lot more hellish with her still living in town, but none of his original reasons for wanting to end their relationship—none of them had changed. He had to stay firm.

He tilted his chin up, stared back without answering.

Katy's expression grew incredulous. "That's it. You're going to remain Mr. Silent and not change a damn thing, aren't you?"

"I never meant to hurt her. And I mean that."

He went back to his task of packing, Katy sitting silently beside him. And the longer she sat there without saying anything, the more he understood exactly how annoying silence could be.

Only there were no words that were going to make this better. He'd stay in his silent prison, and eventually the numbness would ease the pain.

JANEY POPPED open the box top to grab a bowl, slopping cereal and milk into it and hitting the living room for supper.

Her new apartment was crowded with furniture and boxes, none of it put in place yet. The guys helping her move everything in hadn't said much, just silently unloaded her stuff then left.

Everyone in the downtown knew Len had as good as dumped her, and it was as if everyone was holding their breath waiting for the explosion to come. She wasn't going to blow up, though.

She'd gone so cold inside there was nothing left to burn. Thinking there had been more between them than there was had been a mistake, and it was time to move on.

Without Len.

Her phone rang, and instead of ignoring it like she'd been for the past week, she answered. "Yes, I'm still alive."

Shannon made soothing noises. "Hell, of course you are. I'm calling to let you know we're coming over. We gave you the room you asked for. Now, you have to put up with us and let us in."

This was the moment that any day of the last week she would've made some excuse to brush them off, but Shannon was right—they'd given her time alone to get her head straightened out like she'd asked. Time to push it into the past.

No more moping around because Len Thompson had cut out her heart and stomped on it. "If you bring food, I'll let you in."

"That's my girl," Shannon said. "Chinese or pizza?"

Janey made a face at her bowl and the now soggy Cheerios floating under the surface of the milk that had gone warm. "Anything you guys like. I have pop in the fridge."

"Screw the pop, Liz is bringing over the hard stuff."

"You are true friends."

Janey dumped her mushy cereal down the toilet, watching the final desperate Cheerio fight for the surface before the water swirled it away. Time to stop moping, definitely, because all the other fabulous reasons she had to stay in town were still there, except for the one.

And obviously *that* had been a lot more one-sided than she'd thought.

By the time the girls banged on her door, she'd cleared room around the coffee table and had music playing on her iPod.

Shannon glanced around, wrinkling her nose momentarily. "Dibs on unpacking the kitchen."

"Janey and me are going to do her bedroom," Liz announced, setting two paper bags on the coffee table. "We've got it all figured out. We work for two songs, then we stop and have a drink."

The sheer determination on her friend's face brought a smile to Janey's lips. "At some point we'll either run out of boxes, or we'll be so tipsy we'll be falling into them."

"Then we'll crash on your couch. It won't be the first time," Shannon said.

"It won't be the last, either." Liz lifted a bottle in the air. "I can't think of anything I'd rather be doing on my Friday night than spend it with friends."

The momentary rumble of pain that struck was shut down instantly, because that was the only option. Friday nights were not about Len anymore, they were going to be a whole new adventure heading forward.

With friends helping, the burden of unpacking was reduced to a doable task. Janey paused to look out the window of the apartment, still momentarily surprised to see city streetlights instead of the green grass of her backyard.

Her world had changed, and she just had to get used to it.

"You've got everything in place with the new job?" Shannon asked.

Janey nodded, turning back to see her friend carry in the final armful of clothing for the closet. "Brad and I worked out a schedule. We've got the legal stuff all done up, and we're booked solid for three weeks straight, and that's without doing any advertising."

"Or adding in managing the emergencies here at the apartment," Liz pointed out. "I think you ended up with a damn good situation."

Janey had to agree. "It's a little strange not being solely in charge of my time, but this is far more practical for the long run. And Brad has turned out to be awesome to work with. I can't believe I thought he was a stick in the mud."

Shannon raised a brow. "Do I detect a note of interest in your voice?"

Janey was liquored up enough to let a loud burst of laughter escape. "Oh, hell no. I'm glad he's a hard worker, but I'm not looking for anyone right now. Not like that."

Her friends exchanged glances before turning back with knowing smiles. "Sometimes the strangest things happen just out of the blue," Liz suggested.

Janey shook her head. She was moving forward in other areas, but it was going to take longer than a few days to get over Len. "If it happens, when it happens, that's fine. But right now, I'm excited about settling into town properly. I always thought I'd be leaving at some point, so it's nice to be able to set down roots for good."

Shannon patted her on the shoulder, and they turned back to the living room, Liz raising the bottle in the air.

"I think it's time for a classic movie," Shannon suggested. "Now that we've arranged your living room into the ultimate television-watching experience."

Janey snickered as she glanced around the crowded space. "The ultimate? We need to work on your life experiences."

Her friend clicked her tongue. "Only three steps between the refrigerator and the couch? Sounds like my idea of heaven."

She grabbed the control and went searching for one of their favourite movies, and as Janey settled on the couch with junk food spread on the table at their feet, she took a deep breath and faced the future.

And tried to ignore the part inside that insisted on wondering what Len was up to that night.

THE LIST of solid, logical reasons he'd thought buying Janey's house was a good idea escaped him. What he felt was numbing pain, and all he saw was carrying on into the future, day after day, with nothing to bring him happiness.

And every new day would simply be a repeat of the one before. Something constantly missing from his life.

The worst was down at the shop. As if they'd talked about it ahead of time, not a single one of his brothers came forward to call him a stupid shit. Maybe if they had they could get the lingering tension over with sooner, but instead work went on as usual. Repetitive jobs were completed day after day accompanied by a bit of the joking—none of that had vanished. Len remained silent, not usually a big part of it anyway, staying on the fringes.

Until the guys would suddenly pause in the middle of whatever they'd been joking about, as if remembering *he'd* done something they didn't understand, and everything would go silent for long enough to be awkward before they turned back to their jobs.

Only his typical silence spared him from getting harassed by people all over town, but he got the *looks*. And the looks were powerful.

He stopped in at the café for lunch. Tessa seated him and handed him a menu without even flirting. "Specials are on the billboard."

"Just a regular," Len ordered.

Tessa stomped off without a word, and Len stared out the window at the rain-wetted sidewalk. This wasn't what he had thought would happen.

When Janey stepped outside of the hardware store across the street, his eyes followed her, greedily soaking in the momentary sight like an addict craving a hit.

Across from him the bench seat made a noise as his brother Clay joined him. "Do you mind?"

Len shrugged.

VIVIAN AREND

He put in his order, and then seemed to become absolutely obsessed with his coffee cup, stirring slowly as he stared into the liquid.

"Something up?" Len finally asked.

His brother nodded. "I've been trying my damnedest to come up with a reason that makes sense for what you did, but I can't figure it out."

It wasn't the greatest of places to have this conversation, but at least they were finally having it. "I just wanted the best for her."

Confusion still covered Clay's expression as his spoon clicked against the ceramic cup. "See, that is what I expect from you—to treat people right, and try to do right by them. That's who you've always been up until now, but this was a totally screwed-up move that makes no sense."

"She was going to leave town," Len offered.

Clay sighed. "Yeah, well, that one seems to have backfired on you big time."

Len nodded. Didn't say anything more.

Clay lifted his gaze to Len's, and heavy sadness shone in the depths. "Look. It sounds like you and her got a bit confused in terms of who wanted to leave town, who was hoping to stay in town, and what you wanted compared to what you thought you were going to get. It's all tangled up, and at this point it really doesn't matter how it got that way. What matters is getting it untangled."

"Maybe untangling it isn't the solution," Len offered.

That one made his brother sit back in shock. "Because everything is so fantastic the way it is?"

Len stared out the window. "We'll get over it."

"Damn stubborn bastard," Clay muttered. He reached across the table, catching hold of Len's wrist. "I don't know exactly why you're insisting you don't care about the woman, but you're not thinking straight. Crazy asshole—you're living in her damn house. How frickin' twisted is that? Can't you see what's happening? You have a chance here for something that's amazing, and you're throwing it away without a fight. Don't do that. Don't fucking give up just because you have some strange idea you two not being together is a good thing."

"I don't want to talk about it anymore," Len insisted even as he had to silently agree. Living in her house was hellish. There were too many memories around him of Janey just from the short time they'd worked together. It was totally fucked up, and the moments he thought he smelled her hand cream or her shampoo were enough to send his heart pounding.

His head aching with regrets.

He was living with ghosts of his own choosing, yet maybe he could change it all if he'd just...

Tessa dropped a plate in front of Len with a lot more force than needed. Clay let the conversation go, at least while they ate their meal.

But once they left the café, Clay picked up the topic again, stepping in front of his brother without any qualms about getting in the way. "Someone once called them 'missed opportunities'. Those times you have a chance to do one thing, and you decide, for whatever reason, to do something else. Maybe you figured it was the best for both of you. Maybe you're scared things were going too fast. Or you were scared they couldn't last. But I'm going to level with you right now, whatever your issue with you and Janey, *don't* miss this opportunity. Maybe it's gonna take some work to untangle things, but if you don't try, you're always going to regret it. And some opportunities only come along once in a lifetime."

Clay seemed to be focused somewhere off in space, and Len wondered if he was talking from experience. He sounded desperate to push Len in a new direction.

Only it wasn't that easy.

All the advice, added to the pain that struck every time he saw Janey on the street—all of it rustled together in his brain, and drove him to sleepless wandering.

One night. The next. Like he'd wandered into a trap, and couldn't find his way out.

Again he walked aimlessly through the house. Signs of all the work she'd done only made the pain burn more. But he'd been the one to screw things up, and no matter that Clay had told him things could be untangled, Len didn't think they could.

He stared at the boxes piled in the living room and listened to the silence echoing through the empty rooms.

A sudden knock on the door shocked him upright. When his father stepped in, Len rose from where he'd been sitting in the dark. "Dad?"

Keith Thompson stared back for a beat before shaking his head, glancing around the box-filled space. Only a faint glow from the streetlights lit the room. "Good grief. What the hell are you doing?"

He flipped on the lights, and Len glanced away for a moment. Looking around and trying to see the place with new eyes, but the only thing in his head was an image of Janey dancing down the hallway toward him wearing that dangerous miniskirt, a slow smolder in her eyes.

"I thought if I gave you a while, you'd be ready to give me a tour." Keith Thompson glanced around again. "I must be working you too hard down at the garage. If you need a hand, you know you only have to ask."

Len nodded. "Just not sure what I'm doing yet."

"That about sums it up, from what I hear," Keith agreed. He stepped closer, moving until he was eye to eye with his son. "I know I'm only your dad, and it's none of my business. But what the hell happened with you and Janey?"

Trust his dad to be the first one to straight out ask him. "I don't want to be with anyone forever."

Shock registered on his dad's face. "You're not serious. You're going to have to explain this one a little better, because you and Janey were about perfect together. In fact, kind of reminded me of those early days when I was courting your mom. We got along so well, and yet it was never boring."

Another spike of pain returned. "That just tells me even more we don't belong together. I couldn't take it."

Len slammed his lips together, having said more than he intended.

Keith Thompson frowned. "You couldn't take what?"

Len waited in silence.

His dad waited longer.

The quiet built between them until it was a living thing. Pulsing and demanding to be fed. It appeared Len came by his stubbornness honestly. He shifted his feet uneasily and finally lifted his gaze to meet his father's.

Keith folded his arms across his chest and nodded once. "I'm serious now, you want to be a stubborn ass and screw up your life, that's one thing, but you answer my question first. You couldn't take *what* that you shoved that girl from your life so hard she's still spinning?"

The words flew out like they were jet-propelled. "Rather shove her out now than lose her down the road and let it tear me apart."

It was like a light went on as Keith Thompson put two and two together. "Oh my God, son. Is this about me losing Meg? About our whole family losing her?"

Len turned away to stare into the darkness of the backyard. "You still aren't yourself," he said. "I still see you reaching out at times for her, and I see the darkness that fills your eyes when she's not there. It took you years before you smiled after she died." Len shook his head. "I'm not strong enough to take that. I'm not strong enough to go through it again."

"So instead you're letting the woman you love think you don't feel anything for her? That makes no sense, because while it hurt like hell to lose Meg—and you're right, it *still* hurts like hell at times—I had all the good moments with her. I had all of those brilliant touches of joy I never would have experienced if I'd been afraid of the pain."

Len could barely breathe. "But you said it wasn't worth it."

Keith swore. "When did I tell you that? Back when she was suffering, and I was surrounded by a cloud of despair, fighting to keep five kids from crowding into hell after me? When nothing made sense and there was nothing I could do to stop the pain from destroying her body?

"Or was it some time when I'd had a couple to numb the pain? You know, maybe that's not the time to be taking a person's word as canon for your life."

Len wanted so badly to believe there was hope, but...

Clay's words echoed. *Don't give up.*

Katy's annoyance with him echoed as well, along with her earnest reassurances. *Janey's got a big heart— she'll forgive you.*

In front of him his father stood like a beacon, drawing him forward to a place of hope. "It's worth it, Len. It's worth the pain to experience the joy."

God.

Len's heart pounded harder. The bands he'd placed around it were cracking at the seams. He'd kept himself separate for all those years. Tried to stop it from happening, but he hadn't been strong enough.

He couldn't miss the opportunity. He wasn't brave enough to live without her anymore.

Only the anger and the frustration Janey had shoved at him in response to his actions burned in a brand new way. "I hurt her. So damn bad," he whispered.

"You loved her damn hard first, though." His dad laid a hand on his shoulder, the heavy weight grounding Len in one place so he could organize his chaotic thoughts. Keith squeezed his fingers. "Am I right? Son, I think you've loved that girl forever. She's always been the one for you."

"What have I done?" Len stared at his father in panic as the truth sank into his soul. He'd caused them both so much pain trying to avoid what was completely unavoidable.

His heart had always belonged to Janey.

His dad was right. Right now he knew being without her was pretty much the worst thing ever.

Keith shook his head as he answered the question. "You were a damn Thompson fool. I've been one more times than I wanted over the years, and you know what? Your mother always forgave me."

There were memories in his eyes as he traveled into the past. Sorrow on his face, but joy as well.

A massive knot blocked Len's throat as he made the confession. "I'm scared I fucked up too bad to be forgiven."

His father squeezed hard, his expression crinkling into the faintest of smiles. "That's the amazing thing about the women we love, Len. They tend to be a hell of a lot smarter than we are. They know we'll make mistakes, and they're willing to forgive us far too often. Only secret is?"

Len waited.

His dad nodded slowly. "You gotta shoot straight with them. Be honest, and *admit* you're a fool. That goes a hell of a long way."

"Means I've got to tell her that."

"Well, she knows you're a fool," Keith pointed out. "You need to get her to tell you how not to be a fool going forward. If you've got enough reasons to offer her why you should be together, it will help."

The room was still dark, and his soul was still curled up tight in pain. But somewhere deep inside, his father's words lit a spark of hope.

Did he and Janey belong together? As far as he was concerned the answer was yes—and had been for a very long time. No matter that fear still lay like an icy ball in the pit of his gut. Janey had enough fire to melt it, if he'd let her.

Now? He had to find a way to convince Janey to give him a second shot.

Chapter Fourteen

ONCE HE made the decision to move forward, Len found himself in undiscovered territory.

He'd never been the aggressor in their relationship.

And from everything he gathered while talking with Katy on the sly, when she wasn't staring at him with that look of total disapproval, he'd hurt Janey hard. This wouldn't be a walk in the park, and in some ways he was glad.

It wasn't chastisement for his soul, but a chance to really appreciate every step along the way. To appreciate the woman Janey had become while somehow making up for having stomped on the precious thing she'd offered him—her heart.

The first time he planned to track her down, he broke away from work a few minutes before noon, hoping to catch her on a lunch break as well.

Clay stopped him before he could silently escape out the back door. "Where you think you're going?" he demanded.

Len's usual response would've been to not say anything, and he was really tempted, but the truth was Clay had given him a shove in the right direction, and his brother needed to know it.

Besides it was good practice for telling Janey things he'd discovered were important.

"I'm going to go grab hold of an opportunity I nearly let slide."

His brother's eyes widened, then he pulled the door open and gestured with his head to the outdoors. Only he placed a hand on Len's shoulder before he could escape, giving him a serious glare. "You hurt that girl again, and I'll work you over until you can't stand. She deserves better than what you did to her."

Len agreed. "She deserves far better than me, but hell if I'll let anybody else have her."

"She deserves *you*, when you're not being an asshole," Clay corrected him. He gave Len a rough pat on his back before shoving him out the door.

Now he needed a little more luck. He phoned his sister and hoped she was in a forgiving mood as well. "Do you know where Janey is?" he asked.

"Maybe I do, maybe I don't." He could all but hear her anger snapping over the line. "Don't know why I'd tell *you* anything about where she is."

Len laid it on the line. "I want to get back together with her."

Once again he got the silent treatment for long enough to make him sweat. Finally Katy came back online. "I swear if you hurt her again, I don't care if you are my brother. I will hunt you down."

"Take a number. A lot of people want my head on a stake."

"Bastard."

"Katy, I miss her so hard."

"*Awwww*. You're such a shithead it took you this long to figure it out. But fine, she's working on a fence down on the four hundred block. I think she said she'd be there all week."

"Thanks."

"And, Len?" Katy warned. "I know it's like pulling teeth for you to open that mouth of yours and say stuff, but you'll have to do more than simply show up. It's going to take a lot for her to trust you again."

The warning had been expected, but he got the full impact of it when he pulled up in the back alley behind her truck.

Another man was holding a fence panel in place while she secured it, laughter ringing out between them. For one evil second a horrid slash of jealousy raced through Len as he walked rapidly toward them.

Janey glanced towards him, and the light went out of her eyes, her laughter dying away. "Len."

The man turned as well. Brad Jons offered him a sour expression and stern face. "What're you doing here?"

Len gestured. "Just wanted to talk to Janey for a minute."

"She's busy," he snapped.

"It's okay, Brad. Give me a minute." Janey stepped toward the front of the truck, turning to face Len with her arms crossed over her chest. "What do you need?"

He wanted to say *I need you*, but it was too soon, and there was a huge lump in his throat. He was intensely aware of Brad refusing to leave to give them privacy.

And yet...in one way he'd rejected her in front of everyone. He would have to prove himself in front of everyone before this was all over. "I want to see you."

Janey looked away, only her eyes weren't focused on anything. "I'm right here. You can see me fine."

"You know that's not what I mean."

"I don't know what you mean a lot of the time," she said quietly. She turned back, her dark eyes sad but determined. "If you don't have anything specific you need from me, maybe you should leave."

"Let me take you out for supper," Len asked. "We need to talk."

She shook her head. "I don't think we have anything to talk about."

She stepped away, back to the fence. Picking up her tools and going back to work.

Brad stared for another moment, as if double-checking to make sure Len didn't plan to do anything foolish, and then he went back to work as well, stepping in and helping Janey adjust the angle on the next set of boards with an easy camaraderie.

Len paced back to his truck with a heavy step, and even heavier heart, and a hell of a lot more determination.

Okay. So it was going to take a little more effort to get things started. Janey had pursued him for years, constantly getting underfoot until she got under his skin. If it had worked for her, he could damn well take a lesson from her determination.

Operation Stalk Janey began in earnest.

It wasn't his usual method, and Len felt awkward as all get out. But the idea of never having her in his arms again was unbearable.

His father had been right. The kind of pain it was to walk down the street and see Janey across the road from him, smiling with her friends, or even sitting quietly and knowing that he wasn't welcome to go talk to her.

That was an even worse kind of agony.

Whatever it took. All of the energy he'd used to avoid her for years, all the strength he'd accessed in the other decisions in his life to resist relationships and resist connections— He took all of that and put it toward getting the one thing he could not live without any longer.

Janey.

If it meant he had to bare his soul, he'd do it. If it meant he had to beg for help from every one of his family and friends, he'd do that too.

And if it meant he had to give her everything within him so that she knew he wanted every bit of her...

He wasn't going to stop. Ever.

SHE WAS being watched, and by who wasn't a mystery, because no matter where she went, it seemed Len was somewhere in the area.

After that first day when he'd asked for a chance to talk, Janey had gone home and cried herself silly. She wanted so badly to say yes, but the hurt inside wouldn't be erased by some well-meaning conversation.

She'd told the truth. She was worth more than he'd given her, and until he found some way to be completely upright and truthful, there wasn't much point in starting another conversation.

Loud knocking sounded on the door of her apartment. She groaned as she got off the couch, all her muscles aching from the cleanup job she and Brad had done at the local Legion. She put her eye to the peephole, sighing as she spotted Mitch.

She pulled open the door. "I don't want to jump to any conclusions."

"I think you're safe in jumping to a few." Mitch grinned, pulling a bouquet of flowers out from behind his back and holding it out to her. "Len figured you'd either slam the door in his face or not open it in the first place. I got deputized to deliver these."

"I'm telling Anna you're giving flowers to other girls," Janey teased.

Mitch's eyes widened. "Oh, your sense of humour still lives."

She shrugged. "*You* didn't do anything that makes me want to stab you in the balls."

He shifted involuntarily on his feet, presenting the bouquet again. "I'm very glad I didn't. But in spite of my brother managing to be a fool, I really think he's changed. And you should take these."

It was too much. Janey shook her head. "I appreciate you stepping up for him, but flowers don't make a difference here."

His grin only got wider as he pulled them back to his chest. "And I said that's what you would say. Thanks. You just won me twenty bucks."

In spite of the tightness in her chest Janey laughed. "You're terrible."

"It's worse than you think. Before I came over here, I made Len agree to do all my dump runs for the next three months." Mitch shifted his shoulders. "Look. I screwed up big-time with Anna, thinking I knew what was best for the two of us. And the best thing she ever did was forgive me for being stupid, before proving to me how good we were together. I hope you give Len another chance."

She held on to the door tightly. "You can take the flowers to Anna."

He nodded slowly, looking as if he wanted to say more, but then he turned and walked away, the broad width of his shoulders stretching his leather jacket, the oh-so-familiar Thompson step taking him down the hall. He could've been Len's twin. A shot of sadness hit.

Along with a teeny, tiny ray of hope.

Janey knew the Thompson family. She knew exactly how stubborn the boys all were, and the only way Mitch would've shown up at her door was for Len to have talked long and hard. It was a move in the right direction. Or at least a step—because talking was a whole lot better than staying silent.

Mitch outside her door was only the start.

After the flowers came the presents. Little gift bags hanging on her truck antenna and on the doorknob of her apartment. Small candies and scented candles. A book of puns.

A distinctly pink bag showed up, hanging off the fence boards when she and Brad came back from a coffee break. Janey glanced up and down the back alleyway, but no one was there.

Brad looked torn between amusement and concern. "If you want me to tell him to get lost, I will." He got the bag off the fence, slowly holding it out toward her. "Or you can tell me to get lost if I'm out of line."

She took the bag, clutching it tightly as she debated what to do. "It's fine."

He waited then asked, "Does *it's fine* mean you guys are together again?"

"No, nothing like that." She peeked inside to discover a small notebook with a pen, tucked in next to a scented candle.

She slipped the package onto the seat of her truck and got back to work, but the entire afternoon, curiosity burned a hole in her brain.

It wasn't until she got home that she discovered the notebook wasn't blank. She turned to the first page to find Len had written a single line.

You wore a blue dress to your graduation.

She paused, thinking back. Holy cow, he was right.

She flipped through the pages to see what else he'd written inside. More notes, in his barely discernible handwriting.

You dyed your hair green once. I wanted to call you a leprechaun, but didn't want you to be upset.

You take relish and ketchup on your hamburger, but no mustard.

She read through them slowly, the tightness in her chest moving into her throat as her eyes grew wet with frustration and fear.

Why did he have to go and be so adorable after she'd decided she didn't want to have anything to do with him? She put the notebook down without finishing, clicking on the television and trying to lose herself in a mindless sitcom.

She missed him so much every part of her hurt. Being torn apart had only shown exactly how much time with him had meant. And his attempts now seemed to be earnest.

But she wasn't accepting anything but total surrender. She still wanted him to be...*him*, it wasn't that. But she needed *everything* if she was going to offer him a second chance.

She glanced at the small, very pink notebook, picturing him going into the dollar store to pick it up, and caught herself smiling.

It was so hard to trust, but if she didn't try, she'd regret it.

Katy was right. Some things were worth fighting for, and her happiness was definitely one of them. As stupid, and as stubborn, and as silent as Len Thompson could be, she'd never been happier than in his arms.

She might be willing to take the chance to get hurt if it meant she got to bask in his fire.

Chapter Fifteen

THE EMAIL arrived first, followed by the message on her phone. Len trying to set up a date with her for that upcoming Saturday night.

She played back the message just to hear his voice. And then she read the email and replayed the message, and cursed herself for being a fool.

It was dangerous territory, but she had to take the chance. She sent back a note, suggesting he call to make the arrangements.

Her phone rang about twenty seconds later.

"Hey."

"Hi, Janey. I've missed you."

She just about spit in surprise, his admission was so unexpected. "It's good to hear you," was as far as she was willing to give at this moment.

"I don't have anything fancy planned," Len confessed. "I want to go somewhere we can talk in private, but I want you to feel comfortable. Not trying to push you too hard, but what I have to say isn't the kind of thing to discuss in a restaurant."

She agreed completely, but the fact he'd thought that through *and* shared his reasons continued to shock her. "You want to go for a walk?"

"Yeah." He hesitated as if there was a lot more he wanted to say, but the only thing he added was when he'd pick her up. Janey sat and stared at the phone in her hand for the longest time, trembling with hope this would somehow work.

The days until their date seemed endless. Time had never passed so slowly before in her life. Not even when she was little, waiting for Christmas, or her birthday, or any other far off, life changing event.

As if fate was determined to drag out every agonizing second.

She was waiting for him outside the apartment house when he drove up. She didn't get a chance to open the door before he was out of the driver side and around, standing eagerly at her side, and yet adorably awkward as he seemed not to know where to put his hands.

"You look great," he said.

His eyes said a whole lot more. He couldn't stop looking at her as if he'd been starving, and she was the only source of sustenance on the planet.

Len wore a faded pair of jeans, another one of his T-shirts stretched to the limit over his muscular chest. Janey swallowed hard to stop the moisture in her mouth from escaping and making her look like a drooling fool.

"Thanks."

He caught her fingers in his to help her into the truck, and she was weak enough to not even protest that she could get in on her own. She was already seated when she finally realized which truck he had brought.

"Oh, God, you got it done." She ran a hand over the smooth leather seat and leaned forward to admire the old-fashioned dashboard.

"This past week," Len said. He handed her the keys. "Slide over and drive."

Janey didn't hesitate. She moved as he crawled in to take her place on the passenger seat. But just because she reacted instantly didn't mean she wasn't aware of how big his offer was.

The smile she offered him was very real. "I promise to be really careful with her."

He nodded, looking forward as he did up his seatbelt. Then he seemed to check for a second, and turned to face her. "You're always careful with the things that are important to me. I trust you."

Oh, well. An instant rush of emotion hit at his words. Janey paused in the middle of putting the key to the ignition. "Are you going to keep surprising me all night long?"

"Are you good surprised or bad surprised? Because that will make a difference how I answer," he drawled softly.

She took a deep breath. "Good surprised, so far."

He nodded and sat back and stared ahead at the street.

This time it didn't seem as if he was ignoring her. More as if he was giving her some space to figure out where everything was and not feel pressure as she started the engine and pulled into the traffic.

A little stiff in the suspension, but Janey was enjoying herself too much to complain.

When she drove the truck into the parking lot nearby the bonfire pit, it was Len's turn to give her a surprised glance.

She held the keys to him. "I haven't been back here since the start of summer, and I kind of missed most of the bonfire that night. Do you mind?"

Len shook his head. He pulled a box of matches from the glove box. "Give me a couple minutes and I'll get a fire going." He gestured to the back of the truck. "Let me grab the box I've got back there."

Janey followed him, sitting on the bench as he fiddled with kindling and newspaper, getting a flame going before he leaned back. He eyed the bench across from her, and the one to her side.

"I can't believe how awkward this is." Janey adjusted her position to leave room for him beside her, facing him as he settled his bulk within touching distance, but not too close. "We've been around each other for years, and we've been a whole lot more than friends. We should be able to handle this."

Len reached slowly for her hands, as if hesitant to touch her without permission. "Just because we've known each other for a long time doesn't mean I can't screw up. I don't want to add any more mistakes to my ledger."

His fingers tangled in hers, his thumb rubbing slowly over the back of her knuckles.

"I can handle awkward. You just need..."

But there was no *just* about it. It was so much she needed, as long as he was willing to give.

"I've always liked you," Len confessed. "I mean, when you were little it was more about enjoying how much you annoyed my brothers, and how much Katy loved you. And when you got older, not only an annoying teenager, I always thought it was like watching happiness in motion every time you stepped into a room."

Janey let her breath out slowly. "Wow. You're starting right in on the hard-hitting stuff, aren't you?"

He turned to look at the flames trickling around the log in the bonfire pit. "I don't quite know what I need to do to make everything right. I want to show you even though I made a mistake, I intend to fix it."

She nodded slowly before realizing he couldn't see her. Then, the momentary pause was fine because it gave her a chance to put some order to the questions she wanted answers to. Only when she started thinking about them, they all twirled in a circle and refused to settle in any logical order.

Why did he buy her house? Why had he started going out with her, or why had he resisted going out with her in the first place?

"Len, it's not as much a matter of fixing anything. It's more like us both knowing what's important to us, because if those things don't line up, there's no use in us being together."

"You're important to me," he insisted. His gaze met hers, dark brown catching hold of her as he refused to look away. "I was scared to let you in. To put anyone into my life who I might lose."

A flicker of understanding struck. "Your mom?"

Len swallowed, then nodded. "When she was in the hospital, those last days, we took turns making sure she was never alone. Not usually Troy or Katy, but me and the older boys. I didn't have a lot of other things going on, so I went after school. My dad would come after supper, and we'd sit with her and talk. Maybe play a little cards. But I watched her slowly fade away."

"It must've been terrible." She'd been old enough to remember the sadness in the Thompson household, and how Katy decided she would take over all the jobs that her mom couldn't do anymore.

There had been an awful lot of macaroni and cheese cooked in that house as Janey had watched the family from the outside looking in.

"Our family changed, but my dad—" Len paused before forcing himself onward. "He'd always been this strong rock I looked up to, and all of a sudden he wasn't only movable, he was falling apart. I came into the room one time to find him sitting there, staring as she slept. Crying his eyes out. I'd never seen him like that before.

"And he started in on how he couldn't lose her. Cursing fate, and wanting so much to change things, but there was nothing he could do."

206

Janey's throat had gone tight. She squeezed his fingers encouragingly. "You don't have to tell me more."

"I do," Len insisted. "Because it all started back then. Couple days later when I was in the room with her alone, she caught me by the hand. She told me, 'It's easier on my side. At some point my pain will be gone, but you're all going to have to deal with it. I'm sorry for that.' I tried to tell her that was crazy, but she looked me in the eye and said that when it was time to go, she didn't want anybody to use heroic measures to save her. 'I'm afraid your father can't say goodbye, but he's got to. It's the only way.' And it was only a few days later when—"

She couldn't bear it any longer. Janey wrapped her arms around him, offering him strength so he could finish.

"You remember all this?" she asked.

He nodded, his face tight as he controlled his emotions. "Like it was yesterday."

He slipped his arms around her as well, the familiar grip of his embrace soothing the aching hole in her heart. She waited, not wanting to push him, not wanting him to stop before he'd gotten it all out.

His chin rested on her shoulder and he spoke softly toward her ear. "I was in the room when it happened. She kind of looked at me and smiled. A sad sort of smile, but then the tension went out of her face like the pain was gone, and that's when she died."

Janey stroked his back gently.

"I didn't do anything. I could've called for help. I could've hit the button for the nurses. But I didn't because she'd asked me not to. There was no way my dad could have done it—let her go—so I did it for them."

Pain wrapped around Janey's heart like a wire of spikes. Pain for the fifteen-year-old who'd been alone with a choice that wasn't one he should have had to make. A choice that another person with a different heart could have handled easier.

How much it must've hurt Len to make that decision. It explained a lot about how he was, and why he held back.

She pulled away far enough to cup his face in her hands. "You didn't do anything wrong. You were showing love the best way you could."

He nodded. "It still changed my world. I think what I did was right, but it still changed me. Heck, for a while I wondered if I would get arrested for not calling anyone."

"Oh, Len."

"I know now that was a stupid thing to be worried about, but I was just fifteen, and Dad was struggling to keep it together, and there was so much going on at home between all of us kids dealing with Mom not being there, that I let my fears in."

Explained the whole lot. Janey shook her head. "I'm surprised you're not more messed up."

He gave a wry smile. "Messed me up plenty. That was part of the reason why I never got involved with anyone. At first it was I couldn't bear the thought of getting close to anyone when I might get thrown in jail at any time. I couldn't do that to a girlfriend. And then when I knew that it wasn't a case of going to prison, I couldn't let myself risk getting close." He took a deep breath. "Especially not to you, even though I really wanted to."

Janey rested her head on his chest, and they both sat and watched the fire for a few minutes. Dealing with all of the new thoughts swirling in her brain as she put together what he had shared with what she knew of him over the years.

Out of everything she wanted to know, it now came down to a final two questions she was pretty clear in asking.

She ran her fingers over his arm he was using to cradle her against his chest. "Why did we start going out? Back at the start of summer when you cared for me that night? What changed?"

His chest moved under her as he took a deep breath. "You told me you were going away. Up until then, I thought you'd be sticking around Rocky Mountain House, and I didn't want to get involved with you because I knew..."

His voice faded, but she didn't push for him to finish the sentence. "So that's why you bought my house. Because you thought it would get me out of town sooner."

Len twisted her until she was looking up into his face. He tucked his fingers under her chin, his gaze taking in every part of her face as he examined her eyes, her lips. "I wanted you out of town before I started believing that being with you would be worth the pain of someday losing you. I wanted you to move on with your life before I lost my courage and confessed I'd fallen in love with you."

My God. Her heart skipped into her throat even as that tiny flicker of hope burned hotter. "You...love me?"

He nodded. "I know that might be hard to believe, and I've done some stupid things that sure don't make it look like that's what I feel. But it's true. It's always been true."

She couldn't get any words past the lump in her throat. Just sat and stared into his eyes, reading the truth there as he caught his hand over top of hers against his cheek.

She wanted to tell him everything would be all right. Wanted to wipe away all of the pain he'd carried over the years, and drag him forward with her into a happier future.

Now she was the one who was scared. "Oh, Len. I want—"

He slid his fingers over her lips to stop her from continuing. "I'm not a big talker. You're right. Some of that is me, and some of it is too many years of holding everything inside. You told me you deserved more, and you're right. I don't want to rush you into anything. I want you to have some time to think, and I have something to show you."

As much as she wanted to do exactly that—rush forward—he was right about needing some time. "I'm so glad you told me," she said.

"I should've told you earlier."

Janey shook her head. "No more apologies."

He looked down at her lips, and for a moment she was positive he was going to lean forward and kiss her. Instead he straightened, helping her to her feet.

The cool air around them was shocking after the warmth of his body had finally begun to melt the ice around her heart.

He held out his hand, and she slipped her fingers into his. The fire in the metal-sided pit before them had faded to nothing, the small amount of kindling burned down to ashes. Len led her toward the path and they walked slowly along the riverside, this time the silence around them not a barrier, but a place of reflection. Time of healing as he continued to hold her fingers, guiding her along the rough bank, keeping her safe.

It was hard to hold on to the hurt he'd caused when he'd finally laid himself bare and required nothing in return.

They didn't talk much. Not even when he helped her into the truck, and she curled up at his side while he drove them back into town. When he took her to the house instead of her apartment, she still didn't ask him anything.

It was up to him to explain, and now that he seemed to be trying to share, she wouldn't push him to go any faster.

His fingers were tight on the steering wheel after he put the truck into park. "I have something for you."

"Another pink notebook?" Janey teased softly.

A slow smile formed on his lips. "Did you like that?"

She nodded. "Made me cry, looking at all those things you could remember about me. I never knew you were watching that hard, but I should've. You're always watching, aren't you?"

"Watching *you*, yeah." He reached under the seat and pulled out an old-fashioned photo album, the type with sticky pages. He stared at it for a moment before handing it to her.

"What's this?"

He hesitated. "You'll see. I want you to read it on your own. I'll be inside."

Len escaped before she could ask for clarification, striding across the lawn, his long legs eating up the distance as he disappeared around the corner of the house, headed for the back door.

Janey examined the cover carefully, but there was no clue of the contents from the generic golden leaf pattern on the hard cover.

She opened to the first page. "Oh, Len, what have you got happening here?"

Under the first sheet of plastic was a sheet of loose-leaf, like the kind torn from one of the notebooks they used everywhere in the Thompson garage. She stared at it for a minute before figuring out she was looking at her own handwriting from back when she was a teen and had first gotten a crush on Len.

The entire page was covered with her signature, only instead of *Janey Watson*, she'd signed it *Janey Thompson* over and over, the lines of script surrounded by dozens of tiny hearts and butterflies.

A flush rose to her cheeks at the thought of Len finding this, followed hard by a rising sense of incredulous wonder when she realized he'd not only found it, he'd kept it all these years.

She traced her fingers over the lines, the pounding in her heart slowly calming, although her smile grew broader.

She carefully turned the page, eager to see what else he'd given her. The second page made her pause until she realized it was an old timetable from the bus schedule. A couple summers after Mrs. Thompson had died, her and Katy had gone away to summer camp, and when they came back, Len had been the one to pick them up.

Just like the little pink notebook, the pages were filled with memories they'd shared long before they'd become intimate. She drew her fingers down the page where he'd tucked a set of tickets from the last May fair. The day Katy and Gage had tricked Len into taking her on some of the fair rides.

Nothing had happened between them, except— something had. She'd felt a zing of excitement beyond normal. A kind of anticipation and hopefulness as they'd laughed together easily, and she'd caught him smiling at her with real emotion.

She turned the pages one after another until she hit about two-thirds of the way through. For the first time the page was blank except for a note in the middle.

There's room for more memories.

She'd been sitting still in the truck for the past however long it had taken to go through the book, but her heart was pounding as if she'd just finished sprinting.

They had the past. They could have a future.

It all came down to what happened in the next moments, and days.

One more brightly coloured sticky note jutted out a little further down in the book. Janey turned carefully to that page, shocked to find he'd slipped the deed to the house onto the page.

There was a handwritten note attached as well.

I'm not good with talking.

I wrote that down, then looked at the list of all the people I talked to while figuring out how to get you to fall in love with me again, and I realized I can do anything I need to get you back.

Mitch told me not to be stupid and do anything outrageous without checking with you first—he said that was important, and that Anna had taught him that lesson.

Gage told me no matter how long it takes for you to forgive me, or how long I have to chase you for, it'll be worth it. And he said he's got proof of that in Katy and Tanner.

And my dad told me no matter how much it hurts to lose someone you love, it's worth every bit of pain because of the good times and the memories you make.

Katy said you wanted to stay in Rocky Mountain House to be a part of her life and her kid's life. She also said if I hurt you, she would personally skin me.

Clay had something to say. Troy did. Heck, everyone in town has been telling me shit over the past couple weeks.

But none of that matters nearly as much as what you have to say.

So if you need more time, take the truck home and let me know when you're ready to talk. But if you know what you want to say, the door's open.

I'll be waiting. However long it takes.

Janey looked toward the house she'd grown up in. A faint yellow glow shone from the living room windows, but the rest of the house remained dark. Like when they'd come home from a holiday, tired and yet happy, returning to a familiar place where they would unpack everything that had happened before moving on.

Inside the familiar walls Len was waiting. Could she take the chance and move forward?

The weight of the photo album lay heavy in her lap, and she realized he *had* been doing one thing she needed. He'd valued her, far more than he'd ever admitted.

And now that he was willing to share what he was feeling—

How could she not take the chance?

Chapter Sixteen

HE'D LET himself into the house, striding forward to the picture window in the living room to stare at the truck and wonder what was going through Janey's mind.

He'd done what he could. He was scared shitless right now at having handed over proof of how long he'd been obsessed with her.

He hoped it would be enough.

There in the darkness, he closed his eyes and prayed for strength. Prayed for courage. And then he did the bravest thing he'd done in a long time. He turned away from the window and went back into the kitchen and pulled out a box of matches.

The house looked totally different than it had a few days earlier. When he realized exactly what it would take to get Janey back, he'd asked for help.

Walking the fine line between making a good impression and pushing too hard—he'd spent his life hiding on the sidelines so making some grand gesture seemed far too blatant. But Katy had assured him this was right up Janey's alley before swearing if he ever talked about it to her she would scream.

So he crossed his fingers and lit the candles that were scattered around the house. Some in the kitchen, more in the living room. The light bounced off the walls and warmed the darkness as the yellow glow radiated hope.

He went down to the bedroom and lit the few he had on his dresser, looking around the nearly empty room and hoping Janey would come and fill it for him. Fill it like only she could fill his heart

He walked back to the living room and waited.

Sharing about his mom and his past had been hard, but not as hard as he thought. Maybe it was true that time heals all wounds. Or maybe it was that when the other choice—losing Janey now—was so devastatingly hard, long-ago trauma didn't seem nearly so drastic anymore.

He was seated on the couch, staring down at his hands when a single floorboard creaked. He snapped his head up to discover Janey staring, her eyes filled with moisture, her arms wrapped around the photo album he'd been building for years.

She cleared her throat. "I did a damn good job on this floor, didn't I? Got almost all of the squeaks before I laid the new hardwood."

Her smartass comment dragged a smile to his lips. "I knew it was quality construction when I bought it."

She laid the album down on the coffee table and held out her hand. "You need to take me on a tour."

"I'd love to." Len accepted her hand, and the two of them stood there in the middle of the living room grinning at each other like fools.

Thank God she put him out of his misery without dragging it out any longer.

"I want to be with you," Janey said. "And I don't expect you to change all your ways, because you being the big strong silent type totally does it for me."

"I just can't be silent about the important things, right?"

"Right."

She tiptoed closer, wrapping her arms around him and laid her head on his chest.

It was like his heart had walked back into his body.

Len threaded his fingers into her hair and tilted her head back, leaning over to press their mouths together. Kissing her—it was supposed to be tender and soft, but once they connected he couldn't stop. He had missed her so much, and her taste was like a drug roaring through his system.

She all but crawled up his body to cling tightly as he made his way down the hallway toward the bedroom. He tried to tell himself he wasn't making any assumptions, and he really wasn't. But getting his feet to go in the other direction would have been impossible.

He laid her out on the mattress and joined her, side-by-side as they kept kissing. Janey's hands rolled over his body, untucking his shirt, short fingernails dragging up his sides.

She pushed him, and he rolled to his back, breaking for air as she stared down. The candles he'd lit reflected off of the picture on the wall, the warm glow showing the hope in her eyes.

With one knee on either side of his hips, she straddled him. Both hands pressed to his chest as she leaned over and dazzled him with her smile. "You know, I once thought of us as playing the game of tag. And right now, I think it's finally safe to say *I got you.*"

"You've got me for as long as you want me, and even longer," he assured her. "You're never getting rid of me. Never."

She nodded, even as she sat back and stripped away her top, the pale brown fabric of her bra covering her breasts but showing her nipples were already tight.

At least for the second she still wore it, because the material flew to join her shirt on the floor.

"God, you're beautiful. Every single bit of you."

Her smile turned a little smug. "You are pretty awesome yourself, and I'm the only one who gets to know exactly how awesome. I like that. I like that very much."

He had to be the slowest of all bastards that he had to think hard before figuring out what she was talking about.

Admittedly, her breasts *were* distracting him. They were right there in front of him as she leaned forward. He took total advantage and licked the tip of one, sucking her nipple into his mouth as she peeled her pants off her hips.

Using both hands to hold her, he curled up to get a better mouthful, loving the noises of pleasure he dragged from her lips, awed by the fact he knew exactly how to slip his hand down her belly and between her legs to cup her intimately.

He pulled back until they were resting cheek to cheek, his lips inches from her ear. "And you're mine from here on. Part of me is glad you had a good time, and part of me wants to go track down everyone you ever fooled around with and remove their teeth with my favourite pliers."

She laughed, and then he was kissing her, the two of them rolling as he lost his clothing, as he stripped away her pants, and they ended up in the same position all over again. Janey looked down with a sense of power and pride.

"I have two questions," she announced.

Len wanted to protest—his body wanted to protest like crazy—but he reined it in because forever was worth a little discomfort. "Shoot."

She trailed her hands down his chest, tracing designs with her fingernails and making his skin come alive. "Why did you give me the deed to the house?"

No hesitation this time. "Because if you want, it's your house, only this time with me. Together. But if you don't want this place, we'll find another. I probably should do something awesome to make up for being such an idiot the last time—"

She took her hands from his body to hold her palms up towards him. "Whoa. You know, you really need to stop being such a chatterbox."

A snort escaped him. He was back to smiling every time she said something. Kind of the way he'd spent most of his life when she was around.

The way he wanted to spend the rest of his life.

"Second question?"

Her smile turned to sheer sexual mischief. "Do you have any condoms?"

For one panicked second he couldn't remember where they were.

HIS EXPRESSION flew past confusion to near terror. And Janey laughed as she rolled off him, reached for her pants and pulled a condom from the front pocket. She waved it at him before opening the package and resuming her position over his thighs. "I'm glad one of us is prepared."

Everything was coming together perfectly, and in spite of any lingering doubts, Janey chose to take with both hands.

Including right now, and the two hands involved a certain bit of Len's anatomy that had risen between them, thick and long. She couldn't resist tormenting him, leaning over to lick the tip. Loving the groan of pleasure that escaped his lips. The silence that fell when she closed her mouth around him, slipping her tongue along the underside of his cock.

He remained partially sitting, his beautifully defined stomach muscles right there to tease with her fingers as she got him wetter. The taste of him in her mouth was good.

There were so many things she wanted to do. Maybe not for the first time anymore, but going back to perfect their skills. To really know what he liked. Not just in the bedroom, but out of it.

She worked briefly, sucking hard, pumping with her hand as he stiffened to rock-solid under her touch. And while she'd love to take this all the way, she needed him in her body even more. Needed to put aside the pain in her heart and accept their future.

She rolled on the condom quickly before getting back into position. Reaching between her legs to angle the head of his cock.

Len pressed one hand to her lower back, the other buried in the hair at the back of her neck. His fingers closed, and he tugged slightly until their gazes met, his dark eyes eating her up hungrily.

Their bodies pressed together, torsos tight as he guided her hips down, and she slowly surrounded him. His cock stretched her as he rolled his hips and buried himself completely.

The entire time he stared at her, holding her captive with eyes burning with love.

Len wasn't full of words—he'd probably spoken his quota for the next three months, but right then Janey didn't mind one bit.

He was speaking volumes with that expression. With the way he held her, tightly with one hand, the other bringing their bodies into intimate contact again and again as he thrust up.

There could've been a speaker mounted in the corner of the room, but what he was saying as he made love with her would still have been louder than any announcement blaring out at maximum volume.

And she listened. Soaked his love in like a refreshing spring rain bringing new hope.

She curled her hands around his neck and let him take charge of their bodies, staring back into his love-filled eyes. Pouring out her own emotions as best she could.

When he slipped a hand between them, teasing her clit and bringing her body closer to the peak, she gave it all to him.

"I love you," she confessed. "I've always loved you."

The words were a mere whisper. Quieter than the sound of their bodies connecting, his thighs slapping into hers.

But he heard her. Oh, how he heard. If she'd witnessed the emotion on his face before, now it was tripled. As if everything that had held him back was washed away and she was flooded with all the things he'd held on to for years.

She was the center of all his adoration as he kissed her. Continuing to make love to her as he rolled her under him.

She didn't care if she came or not—her world was pretty much as perfect as life could be right then—but in the midst of her joy, pleasure broke. Her body accepted him with delight and held on tight.

A hard gasp stole from his lips as he stopped, deeply connected. Her body squeezing tight around his cock as he came. His hips pulsing against her as if he were trying to get even deeper.

He cradled her like she was precious. He pressed a million kisses over her cheeks and eyes, over her open lips as she couldn't stop laughter from bubbling up.

They lay together afterward, candlelight flickering against the walls, his heartbeat slowing under her ear as she rested her head on his chest. His arms held her tight, and she didn't mind one bit.

There was nowhere she would rather be.

Epilogue

"I LOVE it."

Janey twirled to face Len, damn near bouncing on the spot as she stared into his pleased face.

He shrugged. "It's only a bookcase."

"But you built it." She stood on her tiptoes to plant a kiss on his lips before settling against his body with a contented sigh. "And you painted it candy-apple red. I can't believe you did that."

His big hands rested on her hips, and he shifted her gently against him. "If it makes you happy, I'll paint everything in the house red."

It was so easy to smile. To let the joy inside her bubble up and come out and paint everything she did.

This wasn't her old house anymore. Not only because the renovations she'd done changed the place from where she'd spent time as a child and youth, but now *he* was there as well. Len. His things mixed with hers all around the familiar setting, turning everything into something brand-new as well.

The home was *theirs*.

"Everyone will be here soon," he warned as she snuck her hands underneath his T-shirt to explore.

It was tempting to pout, but then she had so much to look forward today. "And then you'll tell me the secret? I can't believe you've kept it from me this entire time."

Len grinned. And placed his finger against his lips.

She pulled out of his embrace with a laugh, reaching to straighten the furniture they'd moved to put the shelf he'd made into position. "Yeah, yeah, I know, you're the man of mystery."

"I think you'll like it." That's all he would share.

Janey didn't bother teasing any further though. She would know soon enough what he'd been concocting for the past month.

After that night when he told her everything, their world had changed. She could tell there were still moments he was afraid, but now he didn't close himself off from her. Those were the times that he'd sneak up behind her, and she'd find herself wrapped in an enormous bear hug. His arms protecting her as he held her tight and reassured himself all over that she belonged to him.

They were making memories. More mementos had been added to the scrapbook, some of them things she had saved over the years.

Her parents were a little perturbed her move to Calgary had been permanently called off, but they'd made plans to come out for a visit at Thanksgiving, and somewhere in all of it, Janey felt as if she had succeeded in making her point. She was successful. She was happy.

"Hello," a deep voice called. "You want us to bring everything in, or are we picnicking on the deck?"

"Come inside, Dad," Len ordered.

Keith Thompson kicked off his shoes and left them at the entranceway before walking forward and holding out an enormous bouquet of flowers to Janey. "Something pretty for my pretty girl."

Len bumped shoulders with his dad on the way past to hold the door for Katy and Gage. "Stop flirting with my woman," he demanded.

"It's your fault for picking one who's just my type," his dad protested. "Pretty and smart. The best combination."

Katy handed in the car seat, and little Tanner stared up at his Uncle Len with big eyes, his mouth twisted into a round O.

Thirty minutes later Janey leaned on the wall between the kitchen and the living room and watched as the people she loved the most filled their home with their noise and conversation. With their laughter and teasing.

Anna and Mitch were curled up on the couch together talking quietly, Anna still wearing her RCMP uniform. Gage now held the baby and was patting Tanner on the back as he discussed some kind of sporting event with an exuberant Troy.

"It's bedlam in here," Clay complained as he walked in the back door and dropped a couple of bags of chips on the table.

"Then you'll fit right in, won't you?" Katy teased her older brother.

Up at the front of the room, Len cleared his throat, conversation rumbling to a halt as everyone turned to face him.

He looked so uncomfortable that Janey wanted to go and rescue him, but then he caught her gaze. Staring straight at her as he spoke to his family.

"When I came to you and asked for help, every one of you did your damnedest to get me back on the right track. This is my way of saying thank you, because what you shared gave me the best thing I ever could've gotten—Janey."

"Damn right," Katy called out, and the family echoed her in some way.

Len smiled, reaching behind him for some wrapped packages. "There's a catch. You get to open these, but Janey and I get to keep them. Right here." He laid a hand on the empty shelving unit behind him before turning back and looking directly at Janey.

So this was the surprise he'd prepared. Janey waited as he paced around the room, dropping off two or three packages with his brothers and his dad before coming to her side and handing her one.

It was wrapped with bright pink paper and frilly bows and ribbons. "You must be getting tired of being teased every time you go down and buy something else pink," Janey said with a smile.

"It makes you happy. I don't mind."

Her heart fluttered at the words, said so seriously as he wrapped his arms around her and cradled her to his body.

"Len, this is awesome." Anna rose from the couch and came across to him, holding out a framed picture of her and Mitch on their motorcycles, the mountain pass in the background making them look a part of the wilderness, but most definitely a couple. She gave Len a hug. "I had no idea you were doing this."

He tilted his head to the side, and she moved briskly across the room, placing the picture on the shelf before rejoining Mitch.

One after the other the Thompson siblings unwrapped pictures. Some older, some recent. All of them placed with lots of happy conversation on the display shelf that was turning Janey's house even more into a home.

Then Keith Thompson unwrapped a picture that made all sound come to a halt.

The patriarch of the Thompson family swallowed hard.

"I had no idea this was still around." He stroked a finger down the edge of the frame that held a shot of the entire family. "We took that at the start summer, before we found out Meg was sick."

Len laid a hand on his father's shoulder. "Remember how hard it was to get everybody to stand still for long enough to take the picture?"

"I remember everything," Keith admitted.

"We *want* to remember everything," Len offered quietly.

Keith nodded. "We do."

Len slipped his arm around Janey. She held on tight, looking up and hoping he could finish this amazing journey he'd started.

"You want to put it on the shelf for us, Dad?"

It was a silent man who made his way across the room to place the family picture in amongst all the rest standing neatly on the shelves of the bright red bookcase. Like a shot of happiness mixed with a sliver of pain, and somehow all of it together made life that much richer.

Keith turned back and nodded at his son. Took a deep breath and glanced around the room.

Janey looked as well, her heart filling even more as she realized this truly was her family now. Katy's eyes were full of tears, but Gage had his arm around her, supporting her like always, Tanner held between them like a living bit of love. Anna and Mitch sat side-by-side on the couch, rock solid as he whispered something in her ear, her face shining brightly. Clay was staring out the window, sorrow on his face, but strength there as well. Determination.

The entire family was silent for a moment until Troy cleared his throat. "Looks like there's still room for more pictures on there."

"That's the idea. Make some memories, spend some time as a family. Every bit of it is worthwhile, even the parts that are hard." Len got the last words out before his voice failed, but Janey was so damn proud of him.

After everyone had finally left and it was just the two of them, she drew him down to their bedroom, closing the door slowly. She turned, staring up at the man she'd loved forever. Letting him see everything she felt inside—exactly how much she cared for him, and trusted him to always be there for her.

She smiled at him from under her lashes. "You want to make some memories?"

Len answered without saying a word.

The series continues with the full-length novel Let It Ride (Thompson & Sons #3), out later this year.

I hope you enjoyed Len & Janey's story! They will be featured in future Thompson & Sons books. You can read the first book in the series, Rocky Ride, and the tie-in story, Baby, Be Mine now. Books 3 and 4, Let It Ride, and A Wild Ride will be out later this year.

About the Author

Vivian Arend has been around North America, through parts of Europe, and into Central and South America, often with no running water. When challenged to write a book, she gave it a shot, and discovered creating worlds to play in was nearly as addictive as traveling the real one.

Now a New York Times and USA Today bestselling author of both contemporary and paranormal stories, Vivian continues to explore, write and otherwise keep herself well entertained.

Made in the USA
San Bernardino, CA
24 June 2014